3 a.m.

Also by Dallas Woodburn:

There's a Huge Pimple On My Nose
(a Collection of Short Stories and Poems)

(Available at www.zest.net/writeon.)

*   *   *

The author has also appeared in the following books:

Chicken Soup for the Teenage Soul IV
Chicken Soup for the Girl's Soul
Chicken Soup for the Soul: The Real Deal on School
So, You Wanna Be a Writer?
Good Friends Come Along Once in a Lifetime

*   *   *

Dallas's writing awards include:

Gold Medal in the *2005 Scholastic Art and Writing Awards* for her Writing Portfolio
Silver Key in the *2001 Scholastic Art and Writing Awards* for Short Story Writing
First place in *Byline Magazine's* 2004 "New Talent Short Story Contest"
First place for Short Story Writing in the 2004 *Let's Write Literary Contest*
First place in the *California Letters About Literature Essay Contest*
Two-time first-place youth winner in the *Ventura Poetry Festival*

3 a.m.

a collection of short stories

Dallas Woodburn

iUniverse, Inc.
New York Lincoln Shanghai

3 a.m.

a collection of short stories

Copyright © 2005 by Dallas Woodburn

iUniverse books may be ordered through booksellers or by contacting:

iUniverse
2021 Pine Lake Road, Suite 100
Lincoln, NE 68512
www.iuniverse.com
1-800-Authors (1-800-288-4677)

ISBN-13: 978-0-595-35786-4 (pbk)
ISBN-13: 978-0-595-80255-5 (ebk)
ISBN-10: 0-595-35786-5 (pbk)
ISBN-10: 0-595-80255-9 (ebk)

Printed in the United States of America

for Gramps—
Thank you for being my "Monday Guy,"
for sharing stories of your life with me,
for teaching me how to trim a rose,
for being an example of living by the Golden Rule,
and for always calling to make sure
I don't miss the sunset.

Contents

Special Appreciation

to Mom and Daddy. For everything.

to Greg—"Greggie" to me—my younger-but-taller brother. I am so proud to be your "Big Sis." Your cover design for this book rocks! Thanks for being my biggest fan. You are my hero.

to Grandma and Grandpap for treating me like a famous author and calling just to let me know you're proud.

to Mrs. Tania Sussman: as my high school English teacher you introduced me to *Gatsby*; as my mentor you have helped me hone my writing voice; and as my friend you believe in me and, just as importantly, let me know it.

to Mr. Larry Emrich for helping to make my four years at Ventura High School a treasure. You are proof that Principal ends in P-A-L.

to Mr. Dennis Enfield: you introduced me to the theater, took a chance on my stageplay "The 74-Year-Old Rookie," and brought my written words to life on the stage. Thank you for giving me one of the best experiences of my high school years. Even more, thank you for being my friend.

to Coach Bill Tokar for your tremendous support and encouragement, both on the track and—perhaps even more importantly—off it. Thank you for letting me be a part of such an amazing cross-country team. You tell us there's more to life than sports—but, through sports, you teach so many lessons about life.

to Dr. Joseph Spirito for your friendship and guidance. Seven years ago, when you bought my first book, you also pre-ordered a copy of this collection because you said you knew I'd write another book. As always, you were right.

to the Bryan family—"Uncle" Wayne, Kathy, Mike and Bob—for being incredible role models and for inspiring me with your unbridled enthusiasm and never-ending support.

to Linda McCoy-Murray for always making me feel like a Pulitzer Prize winner.

to Zest.net—Ric, Rob, Duane, and staff—for helping a technology spaz like me set up an awesome website (www.zest.net/writeon), patiently listening to my endless computer questions, and always coming up with a remedy that works.

to Nancy Clark, deputy editor at *Family Circle*: thank you for giving me a tour of the office; for lunch at Grand Central Station; and, above all, for giving a young unknown like me a chance. Even though I write my *Family Circle* column from a teen's perspective, you treat me like an adult. I still have to pinch myself!

to Debbie Mitchell, producer at CBS's "The Early Show," for the time you spent pre-interviewing me on the phone, taking care of my plane tickets and hotel reservations, introducing me to New York

City, and for making me feel like the most important guest you've ever booked.

to Hannah Storm for your genuine warmth, for easing my nerves, and for making my brief five-minute national TV debut on "The Early Show" feel like a chat between friends.

to Barry Kibrick, host of "Between the Lines," for your inspirational author interviews and for your kindness in inviting me to watch a taping of your show in the control room of the KLCS-TV studio. You are as truly friendly in person as you seem on TV.

to Jana Pettey, Teri Robbins, and Anna Bolton of *Justine*: thank you for my first magazine publication credit—wow, what a feeling!—and for giving me a voice in your pages.

to Céleste Walker, editor of *Listen*: thank you for letting me know I'm appreciated, and for giving me the chance to express myself in new ways—like a comic strip!

to Kristin Godfrey, editor of *Writer's Digest*: your magazine is a writer's treasure chest. I am honored to be published on your pages.

to Sandhya Nankani, editor of *Writing*: thank you for giving me the chance to share my love for the written word with other passionate young writers.

to all the incredibly talented—and incredibly kind—authors who have taken the time to talk to me and read my work and write back to me: Joan Bauer, Michael Bedard, Elizabeth Berg, Joan Chase Bowden, Karleen Bradford, Niki Burnham, Meg Cabot, Catharine Clark, Sharon Creech, Sarah Dessen, Jennifer Donnelly, Fannie

Flagg, Julia McGuire, Jo Ellen Heil, Valerie Hobbs, Randy Powell, Ann Rinaldi, Tom Sawyer, Laurie Stolarz, Wendelin Van Draanen, and Ellen Wittlinger. You inspire me tremendously and your encouragement means more than you can know.

Lastly, to everyone I may have forgotten to thank due to my temporary brain freeze. I promise I'll make it up to you when I finish my three-quarters-completed novel, *Ghost Fingers*. Thanks for your forgiveness and support!

Foreword

My computer screensaver is a photograph of a six-year-old girl perched at the kitchen table in front of an old-fashioned manual typewriter. She is sitting up on her knees in order to be tall enough to reach the keys. The little girl stares intently at the blank piece of paper in front of her, deep in concentration—oblivious to the camera, oblivious to her father as he snaps her picture, oblivious to everything save for the story unfolding inside her mind.

I am that little girl, now grown into a young woman of seventeen. The picture on my screensaver always makes me smile because I think it captures the essence of who I really am: a dreamer, a creator, a storyteller trying to share with others the magic I've discovered in my own imagination. To say it plainly, I am a writer. For as long as I can remember, writing has been my passion—my *great* passion.

I published my first book, *There's a Huge Pimple on My Nose (a Collection of Short Stories and Poems)*, in fifth grade. *Pimple* is proof that with a lot of hard work, a lot of perseverance—and, yes, a lot of support, too—a small idea can snowball into something bigger than you ever dreamed. My snowball began as a snowflake when I received a fifty-dollar grant from P.A.G.E. (Parents and Advocates of Gifted Education) to write and self-publish a children's book. I also proposed using profits from my book sales to pay back the grant so an extra one could be offered the following year. My first printing, done at a Kinkos copy shop, was modest: twenty-five staple-bound forty-page books. Actually, they were more like thick pamphlets, but no matter—to me, they were books, *my* books, the most beautiful books I had ever laid eyes upon. J.K. Rowling wasn't more proud of her first Harry Potter hardcover edition.

My fellow students and teachers at Ventura's Poinsettia Elementary School, bless them, acted as if *Pimple* was at the top of the New York Times Best-Seller List. The first twenty-five copies promptly sold—*"Dallas, will you autograph it for when you become famous?"*— in a couple of days. Can you imagine what a turbo-boost this was to a fifth-grader's self-esteem? To anyone's self-esteem, for that matter? I was pursuing my dream, but I wasn't pursuing it alone—my family and friends and teachers were right there with me.

So. I went back to Kinkos, ordered twenty-five more books— and soon sold all those as well. After three more trips to Kinkos, where the workers now knew me by name, I searched out a publishing business and ordered 700 glossy-covered, glue-bound, professional-looking *Pimples*. My little forty-page dream evolved from a snowball into a blizzard, with reviews in the national magazines CosmoGIRL! and Girls' Life; booksignings at the Cal Lutheran Author's Faire and the Jack London Writer's Camp in San Jose; a "Dallas Woodburn Day" at the Santa Barbara Book Fair; and being featured as a "real author" alongside famous real authors such as Michael Crichton and Wendelin Van Draanen in the nationally-released book *So, You Wanna Be a Writer?* The Los Angeles Times even raved, "If you simply want to enjoy some remarkable writing, it would be hard to find a book more satisfying than Dallas Woodburn's." I still have to pinch myself, but *Pimple* eventually sold more than 800 copies—to me, it seemed like 800,000!—and I repaid two P.A.G.E. grants.

I have received letters from readers across the nation, and even Canada, saying they can relate to my stories. Many have expressed thanks for helping them get through a difficult time in their own lives. Hearing that I've connected with a reader is, in my opinion, one of the most rewarding aspects of being a writer. But at the same time, I know there are countless individuals who are not affected by my writing in the least—because they truly *cannot* read my words. Illiteracy is a very serious problem in our society today. A recent study conducted by the U.S. Department of Education found that half—HALF!—the adult population (an estimated ninety-million Americans) does not possess the most basic level of reading ability. This in turn leads to a higher likelihood of poverty, crime, and unemployment.

Helping battle illiteracy is one of my lifelong goals. It is why I also used a portion of *Pimple's* profits to found "Write On!"—a non-profit organization to encourage kids to read and write through essay contests, read-a-thons, and an inspirational website (www.zest.net/writeon). By purchasing this book, you, too, are showing your support for youth literacy because a portion of the sales of *3 a.m.* will be donated to my Write On Scholarship Fund to help send a deserving student to a writing camp each summer.

In addition, a couple years after *Pimple* debuted, I started an annual Holiday Book Drive with the motto *"Toys get broken, but books last a lifetime."* In the past four years I have collected and distributed 6,390 new books to underprivileged kids who might not otherwise have received anything for Christmas. (For information about how you can become involved, please visit www.zest. net/writeon.)

Write On's annual Holiday Book Drive brings me the most pride of any of my endeavors. It not only gives books to disadvantaged children—just as importantly, it shows them people care. I have found that many, many people *want* to help others, but often don't know how. My book drive has given them an easy, and meaningful, avenue. It has humbly grown from bringing a few boxes of donated books to my city's local library the first year, to in 2004 collecting and distributing more than 1,600 brand-new books to various local charities including two Boys and Girls Clubs, three libraries, and youth organizations such as Casa Pacifica and Project Understanding. From a one-person effort it has evolved into an entire community of volunteers, with collection boxes at local bookstores, post offices, and fourteen area schools. I have learned that together, we can help give sad tales a happier storyline.

After all, I know firsthand about sad tales turning happy. Born three months prematurely, I weighed a mere two pounds, six ounces, and back in 1987 the chances that I would survive were extremely small as well. A team of surgeons flew to my small hometown of Santa Maria and delivered me by an emergency Cesarean section, then took me to the state-of-the-art Neonatal Intensive Care Unit in Fresno, where I stayed for eight touch-and-go weeks.

On my desk I have a framed photograph of my sickly newborn self, a tiny skin-and-bones infant inside a high-tech Plexiglas incubator and hooked up to an array of medical monitors and wires, tubes and needles. To others, the photograph may come into focus as heart-wrenching and tragic, but what I see is a portrait of inner strength and survival. Indeed, the sickly infant in the faded photo has become my personal cheerleader, silently urging me on through every new challenge—physical, academic, spiritual—I undertake. I know the preemie-who-was-me will continue to inspire the grown-up-me in my journey to become The Female John Steinbeck and make a lasting impression with my heartfelt written words. Too, the preemie-in-the-photo keeps the grown-up-me grounded during the highs of success, and gives me perspective during the low times by simply reminding me how blessed I am to be alive and healthy.

One of the surgeons who delivered me told my dad that May 29th night: "Your daughter is a real fighter."

I guess the doctor was right. Actually, I *know* he was. I was a fighter. I am still. Indeed, whenever I am faced with a challenge, I think about those words—"Your daughter is a fighter"—and I draw strength.

I often need this strength when I sit down to write.

Because in truth, while writing thrills me, it also terrifies me. I fear I will run out of words, or spend weeks on a story that does not blossom. I worry about the infamous "writer's block" that I have experienced firsthand and—trust me—wrestling alligators must be less daunting.

Some of my friends think I'm crazy. Sometimes I think I'm crazy, too. Running on the cross-country team is one thing—"You mean you actually *like* to run?! Doesn't that get boring?"—but at least out on the running trails I'm surrounded by my teammates who are just as looney as I am. Wrestling alligators is quite a different matter. For many of my high school classmates, the worst thing a teacher can say, worse even than "Math test tomorrow," is "In-class essay today." Writing is tortuous—why would anyone do it for fun? Why do I choose to spend hours each day or night with my fingers tapping across—or worse, sitting motionless on—the keyboard, staring at a computer screen?

Why, indeed? I still don't really have an answer. I guess because writing is a lot like running—and not just because it's an activity most normal people regard with eyebrows raised. Running is hard, but—as I learned when I was forced to sit out my high school sophomore and junior cross-country seasons because of leg injuries that eventually required surgery—*not* running is harder. The same goes with writing. Writing is hard—tortuous, tedious, boring, scary. But, for me at least, *not* writing is harder.

So. I am a coward. I take the easier route. I keep writing. And writing. And writing some more. Why? I guess because the thrills are worth it. I may not always enjoy the sometimes-tedious, sometimes-dull, sometimes-terrifying process of writing—but I love the sweet satisfaction of having written. And, you're probably wondering, what do I have to show for my alligator wrestling? It's been a long time since fifth grade; a long time since *Pimple* was published. What have I been up to the past seven years?

Well, I've broken into the nonfiction field, having written articles for numerous national magazines including Writer's Digest, Justine, and Writing, and books including *Chicken Soup for the Teenage Soul IV.* You know what else that forty-page dream has snowballed into? I write a regular "Teen Talk" column for Family Circle magazine (with a circulation of five million readers!) about teen/parent relationships—from a teenager's unique perspective.

More beautiful snowflakes. I tried my hand at playwriting and wrote a three-act script, "The 74-Year-Old Rookie" (you'll find the award-winning short story that inspired it later in these pages). Mr. Dennis Enfield, the brilliantly eccentric drama teacher at Ventura High School, was kind enough to not only take a look at my script—he produced it as our spring play in 2004. What an amazing experience!

All of this has been exhilarating and rewarding, but after seven years I was itching to write another book. It's quite a different collection than *Pimple.* More mature, I think. I guess my writing has grown up with me. In fact, I feel my growth and development as a person can be traced through the growth and development of my writing: from *Pimple*'s childhood poems about peanut butter sandwiches and magical stuffed animals coming to life; to this collection's more complex themes dealing with love, grief, self-discovery and internal awakening. My search for my own unique storytelling voice and writing style parallels my personal journey to find my true inner self and place in the world. Not only has my great passion for writing shaped who I am, it has also shaped my dreams and aspirations: in essence, who I wish to become.

French philosopher Denis Diderot once wrote, "Only passions, great passions, can elevate the soul to great things." I feel blessed to have already discovered my great passion; to know that I want to study Creative Writing at USC (where I will be a freshman "Trustee Scholar" in the class of 2009 this fall) and further pursue my craft. My great passion for writing has inspired me to push beyond self-doubt and take the risk of sharing my words with others—with *you.*

I shared *Pimple*'s success with you earlier—what I didn't tell you about was my "failures." I could wallpaper my bedroom with all the rejection slips I've received from editors. But I am a preemie; I am "a fighter"; I keep writing. And all the while, my great passion for wrestling alligators burns brighter with each sunrise.

Writing has opened so many doors for me. It has given me self-confidence, a means to express myself, and hopefully a path to change the world for the better in some small way. I truly believe the written word is one of the most powerful and important tools in society. With my writing I hope to bring people together, to connect with them, to make them think. As Joseph Campbell writes in his book *The Power of Myth*, writers and poets have the unique job of passing down myths through the generations. There are common themes found in literature, from all societies, races, religions, time periods—threads that link us together as human beings. The writer's job—my job—is to keep our stories alive so these threads continue weaving a tapestry into tomorrow.

I'd like to close my Foreword thoughts with one of my favorite quotes about writing. It's by Emily Dickinson:

A word is dead,
When it is said,
Some say.
I say it just begins to live
That day.

Thank you, dear reader, for giving my words—words I was often up writing at 3 a.m.—a chance to live by letting me share them with you in these pages.

THE 74-YEAR-OLD ROOKIE

(Winner of the Silver Key in the Scholastic Art and Writing Awards)

THWACK!

The ball rocketed off the bat and soared seemingly towards the moon, flying over the outfielder, flying over the chain-link fence surrounding the small vacant lot, flying until gravity finally pulled the leather comet back down to earth in a collision course with an old man shuffling along the sidewalk.

"Hey!" the boy in center field shouted. "LOOK OUT!"

With reflexes that seemed decades younger than his seventy-four years, the old man reached up and…miracle of miracles…the baseball stuck in his hand as though his palm was made of Velcro.

"Wow! Great catch!" the center fielder called out in sincere admiration. "Barehanded, too!"

The old man smiled, but then a sadness quickly washed over his face.

If only Timmy had seen this! he thought to himself. *Why couldn't I have made this catch sixty years ago? Then things would have been different. So different…*

*   *   *

Six decades had come and passed, yet Max still remembered that fateful day as though it happened last Tuesday.

Max saw the baseball flying towards him, saw himself backing up…backing up…just the way he'd seen Joe DiMaggio do so many times in Yankee Stadium. He reached his glove upward and then—YES!—Max felt the sweet, hard smack of the ball landing in the leather webbing. Max, the last boy picked to play, had made the game-winning catch! Looking at Timmy's startled face, Max quickly brought the glove down to see for himself…

…and watched in horror as the ball plopped to the ground. *Oh, no! What have I done?! I dropped it! I DROPPED IT!* Max thought, his inner voice screaming silently in a panic. *My one chance to prove I'm one of the guys, and I blew it!*

Max stared at his empty glove in disbelief, not even thinking to pick up the ball as the batter raced around the bases to score the game-winning run. Max thought things couldn't get any worse. He was wrong. Everyone laughed and jeered at him, even his own teammates. And to Max's horror, no one was laughing louder than Timmy.

"I knew we shouldn't have let you play. I knew you'd blow it!" Timmy sneered as Max tearfully ran away. "You lost the game for us, Mini-Max, you little dweeb! Go on, go home. I think I hear your Mommy calling you. Go away and don't never come back, you hear me!"

✳   ✳   ✳

"Hey, Mister! Aren't you gonna throw us our ball back?" the center fielder called out politely to the old man. "I know it's old and falling apart, but it's the only one we got."

Startled out of his sad trance, Max tossed the tattered baseball back over the sorry excuse for a fence and began to shuffle away, but then halted when he heard the boy yell to him again:

"Wanna play?"

Truth be told, Max had daydreamed many times of joining these boys when he walked past their daily summer baseball game on his way to pick up the newspaper at the corner market. But no, he would just make a fool of himself again like he had sixty years ago. He shook his head fiercely but spoke kindly:

"No, no. Not today, boys, not today."

Max turned back and shuffled home.

"C'mon, Sean, throw the ball in before we all grow as old as him. What's taking you so long?" one of the boys yelled to the center fielder. Max glanced over his shoulder and saw Sean wave to him before throwing the ball back in to the impatient pitcher.

✳   ✳   ✳

Sixty years had faded into sunsets, but the pain remained crimson bright.

The taunting was too much for young Max. Tears streamed down his dirt-streaked face and his nose ran like a broken faucet. He couldn't believe he had ever thought Timmy and The Gang were his friends. He was so stupid! He ran away; away from the park; away from the baseball diamond; away from the hurtful boys still yelling insults at him.

If only for once Max *hadn't* listened to his mother, but of course that was foolhardy thinking because young Max always listened to her.

"Maxie, dear, it's such a beautiful day. Why don't you go play outside with your friends?" she had said. "I hear they have baseball games every day down at the park."

"Aww, Mom, I'm no good. I always get picked last. The boys don't even want me there."

"Maxie, you have to think positively. Who knows, maybe you'll hit the ball as far as...Bob Ruth!"

"*Baaabe* Ruth, Mom. It's *Babe* Ruth."

"Yes, that's him, Maxie. Babe Ruth. See, you know a lot about baseball. I bet you'll do wonderfully, dear. There's probably a slugger inside you just waiting to get out!"

"But Mom, I'm in the middle of the Hardy Boys' latest adventure! I wanna see how it comes out."

"Now, Maxie, you can finish that later. I'm sure those boys at the park would love to have another player. Go on. Dinner's at six. I'll make your favorite—Sloppy Joe Sauce on Noodles—and you can tell me all about how you were the hero of the game. Run along now."

Max reluctantly put down *The Hardy Boys* and got up to leave, but his mother stopped him.

"Wait, Maxie," she said, "don't forget your mitt. And why don't you take the new baseball your father got you for your birthday? That was two months ago and you still haven't used it." She found the baseball gathering dust on Max's bookshelf and wiped it off on her apron before gently tossing it underhand to Max, who—of course—dropped it.

With a heavy sigh and a heavier heart, Max picked up the brand-new ball and left for the park.

＊　　　＊　　　＊

Shuffle, shuffle, shufflle…

With the daily paper tucked under his arm the next day, Max again walked past the vacant lot with the ballgame in progress.

Sean ran up to the fence and called out, "Hey, Mister! Are you gonna play today?"

"Not today," Max said, surprised at the repeat invitation. "But thank you for asking."

Once more the old memories came flooding back.

Unlike Sean now, sixty years ago the boy ballplayers didn't notice Max standing on the sidelines. Not at first, anyway. They were having a grand time, laughing and joking and playing. Oh, how Max wished he was out there with them.

Timmy was just getting ready to unleash a pitch, turning his head to keep the runner on first base from stealing second, when his eye caught Max timidly watching their game. Timmy stopped his delivery and called time out.

"Look who's here, everyone!" he announced. "Mini-Max himself!"

Max, his cheeks hot with embarrassment, looked down at his shoes as all the kids laughed.

Then, to Max's great surprise, Timmy sauntered over, put his hand on Max's shoulder, and said, "We could use a right fielder. Wanna play?"

"Uh, baseball?" Max asked, his brain numb with disbelief.

"Of course baseball, ya dummy!" Timmy snickered. "This ain't no football field, is it?"

"Well, uh, no…no, of course it isn't…"

"Okay then. So are you and your *new baseball* there gonna play, or aren't you?"

"Sure," Max found himself saying. "I'll play."

"Then c'mon already!" Timmy said, putting his arm around Max and tossing the new baseball to one of his pals. "You can be on my team, okay?"

Maybe Mom was right after all, Max thought, beaming.

*   *   *

Shuffle, shuffle, shuffle...

The smallest boy was up at bat when the old man passed by the baseball lot the next day.

"Okay, guys, move in!" the pitcher sneered. "I think we've got this game cinched already." He laughed, and so did his teammates. Old man Max sighed to himself. Some things never changed.

But then again...maybe some things did change after all.

"Shut up, Alex!" Sean yelled to the pitcher. Then—even though he was in the outfield—Sean began to cheer for the scrawny batter. "It's okay, Mikey! You can do it!"

Mikey, however, did not look as confident in his own capabilities as Sean pretended to be. He swung awkwardly once — "STRIKE ONE!" — twice — "STRIKE TWO!" — three times — "STRIKE THREE! YOU'RE OUTA THERE!" hollered Alex.

"It's okay, Mikey!" Sean said. "You'll get it next time. Good game, guys! Let's take a water break." Then Sean glimpsed Max watching through the outfield fence.

"Hey, Mister!" he hollered across the fence. "I'm gonna pick you for my team next game, okay?"

Max wanted to yell "Sure!" and run—or, rather, shuffle as quickly as his arthritic legs would carry him—out onto the field, but he didn't dare. Instead, he shook his head "no" and kept walking, thinking of the awful day Timmy picked him for his team.

"Go out there in right field and hopefully nothing will come your way," Timmy had said. Max, too, hoped the ball wouldn't come his way. He was thrilled just to be on the same field with Timmy and The Gang. He, Max Johnson, was finally one of the guys!

Not for long.

Moments later, Max dropped the pop fly that would have won the game and was banished forever from playing ball with The Gang.

If only the catch I'd made three days ago, lucky as it was, had happened on that fateful afternoon sixty years ago, old man Max thought to himself as he shuffled away. *Then maybe instead of these boys inviting me to play day after day… Timmy and The Gang would have.*

*   *   *

Timmy and The Gang had always teased young Max at school, but after that fateful day at the park their taunting became even more merciless. Timmy would saunter over to the lunch table where Max sat alone, reading a book—usually a Hardy Boys adventure—and steal Max's apple.

"The library's on the other side of campus," Timmy sneered one time, tossing the apple to one of his pals.

"Hey! Give it back!" Max pleaded.

But the boys continued tossing the apple back and forth to each other, laughing at Max's clumsy attempts to intercept it, until eventually Timmy grew bored. "Here," he said, casually tossing the apple to Max, who, of course, dropped it. "Same old Mini-Max," Timmy laughed. "I swear, you couldn't even catch a cold."

The worst part of all was that Margaret sat just two lunch tables away, close enough to hear the whole exchange—and to see Max made to look the fool. Again.

Not that Margaret would ever say anything to Max about it. Along with being the prettiest girl in the whole school, she was also the nicest. She was even nice to Mini-Max, and never treated him like a loser. Truth is, they were sort of friends.

Shortly after the apple incident, when Max was walking home from school, he glimpsed Margaret up ahead. She was crouched down on the ground, gathering up an armload of books and scattered papers and pencils. Max hurried over and helped her pick up the mess.

"Thank you *so* much, Max," Margaret said, smiling her beautiful smile at him. "Clumsy me, I was walking along not paying attention, and I tripped on a crummy crack in the sidewalk and fell."

Max picked up one of her books. "You read *The Hardy Boys*?"

"Yeah, they're the best!" Margaret said excitedly. "I know most girls like *Nancy Drew*, but I don't fancy those books nearly as much. I mean, Nancy always gets in trouble and some big strong guy has to come save her. *The Hardy Boys* are way better, if you ask me."

"Yeah, I love *The Hardy Boys* too!" Max agreed. "I've read the latest book six times! Well, okay—I've read it twice, but it felt like six times. I couldn't put it down—I even forgot to do my homework!"

"I know! I'm reading it for the second time, too. It's the best one. My favorite by far."

Max handed the book to her and continued gathering up the scattered papers. He picked up one of her notebooks and paused for a second, looking at it. The words were out of his mouth before his shy self could think to stop them: "Hey Margaret, did you draw this?"

Margaret looked over and blushed slightly. "Oh, yeah, that's just something for art class. It certainly doesn't belong in a gallery or anything, but I tried my best."

"Yes it does," Max insisted. "It's swell, Margaret. You should frame it. You're a great artist—it looks exactly like you."

"You think so? We were supposed to draw a self-portrait, but I don't think it looks much like me."

"Sure it does! Why…it's almost as pretty as you are!" Max quickly averted his gaze to the ground, not believing he actually said that out loud. "I mean—uh, you're, um, you drew a really good picture of yourself." He could feel his ears turning red-hot as he handed the art notebook to her.

"Thanks, Max," Margaret said. Max wasn't sure if she was talking about the compliment, or about giving her notebook back. *Maybe both,* he thought, smiling slightly to himself.

"Max," Margaret said suddenly. "Can I ask you something?"

"Uh, sure," Max said, caught off guard. "Shoot."

Margaret took a deep breath. "How come you never talk to me at school? I mean, we used to be best friends. Remember, when we were little kids? We played together all the time—we even took naps at each other's houses. But now you ignore me. I don't understand, Max. Have I done something wrong?"

"Done something wrong?" Max was incredulous. "Of course not. What are you talking about? I do *so* talk to you at school." The words sounded lame even to his own ears.

"When?" Margaret insisted, slight agitation in her voice. "When in the last six months have you ever *talked* to me in front of people at school?"

Max was beginning to feel irritated himself. "Well, I help you with your math homework all the time. And it's not like I do it in sign language."

"I know that's just because your mother makes you, Max!" Margaret retorted. "If our parents weren't friends I swear you'd never even say hi to me. You probably wouldn't even have stopped to help me pick up my books just now."

"That's not true at all!"

Margaret's eyes, meeting his, were a combination of hurt and confusion. Max wished he was brave enough to explain the real reason he hardly ever spoke to her anymore. But he couldn't find the words—or the courage.

"I just don't understand why, Max," Margaret continued. "Is it because I'm a girl? You're embarrassed to be friends with a girl now? Is that it?"

"No, Margaret, I—"

"Hey, Margie! Wait up!"

Max and Margaret both turned to see Margaret's friend, Louise, hurrying down the sidewalk towards them. Ignoring Max completely, she grabbed Margaret's arm and began to drag her away. "Margie, hurry!" she said. "The boys are playing baseball down at the park. Timmy's gonna be there! The gang's all waiting. C'mon!"

Margaret gave Max one quick glance before standing up, arms full of her newly retrieved books. Then she was off with Louise, hurrying away to the baseball game to see Timmy. Hurrying away from Max, the nervous fraidy-cat who couldn't even bring himself to tell her how he really felt about her.

Max wondered if he'd ever get the chance again. He sat in the lunchroom, watching Margaret over the top of his book. Timmy sauntered over and sat down next to Margaret and began talking to her.

Max sighed. *Margaret's so nice, she's even nice to a jerk like Timmy,* he thought. *I guess that's just how life is. Girls like cool guys. Ones who can play baseball. Not bookworms like me.* Max turned back to *The Hardy Boys,* but he'd only read a few paragraphs before he was again interrupted.

"Hi Max."

Max looked up from his book to see…

…Margaret standing there. At his table. Saying hello to him.

Max was so excitedly flustered he closed his book without even thinking to put in his bookmark. No matter—*The Hardy Boys's* could wait to solve their crime. "Uh, h-hi, Margaret," he said.

Gosh, she's pretty, Max thought. Her dark hair was pulled back from her face in two barrettes, revealing her warm green eyes.

"Listen, Margaret," Max began, "about the other day—"

She stopped him. "It's okay, Max."

Max racked his mind for something else to say.

"So, uh…do you need help with your math homework?" he asked.

"No. Well, actually, yes," Margaret said with a self-deprecating smile. "But the reason I came over here was…to see if you're going to the backwards dance with anyone?"

"Um-well-no," Max stammered. "I mean, who would ask me?"

"I would, silly. I mean, I *am* asking you. Would you like to go with me?"

Max looked at Margaret in disbelief. *Is this really happening?* he thought. *Maybe Margaret does like me after all! Maybe she doesn't care that I stink at baseball!* Max was about to say yes when he spotted Timmy and The Gang laughing—sneering at him, he knew—from two tables away. From Margaret's table. *Wait a minute…*

Max gave himself a mental kick in the head for being so stupid. When he spoke, his voice was almost a whisper. "No," he said sadly.

*   *   *

"Maxford William Johnson!" Max's mother exclaimed, storming into his room the next day. Max looked up from his book. His mother frowned at him, hands on hips. *Uh-oh.*

"What?" Max said.

"You know what I'm talking about, Mister," she said. "I heard today that you said 'no' when pretty little Margaret Hart asked you to the Sadie Hawkins dance. Shame on you, Maxford. Shame! On! You! Her mother told me she was quiet all day yesterday after you broke her heart. The poor darling! Let me tell you, Buster, just because you are a handsome young man doesn't mean you can go tearing people's heartstrings out! What were you thinking, Max?"

Max's head was spinning faster than the Tilt-a-Whirl at the country fair. *How has this twisted around and become my fault?* "But Mom," he said, "she was just joking…"

"That's not what I heard, Mister."

"You don't understand, Mom," Max sighed. "The kids at school…they just…they just don't like me. Margaret would never seriously ask me to a dance. Someone put her up to it. Timmy, probably. She was making fun of me."

His mother's face softened. "That doesn't sound like the Margaret I know, Maxie," she said. "I think Margaret's really sweet on you."

Why are mothers always so dense? Max tried to get her to understand. "No, Mom, she's not," he said. "She probably likes Timmy. All the girls like Timmy. I bet Margaret asked him to the dance first, and he said he'd go with her only if she *pretended* to ask me, 'Mini-Max The Loser,' and everyone could have one more thing to make fun of me about."

Max studied his shoes, too embarrassed to meet his mother's eyes. She tilted his chin up so she could see his face. "Oh, Maxie," she sighed. "I'm sorry some of the kids at school are like that. But you know what? You just have to ignore them. There are lots more who are nice—you just have to find them. Like Margaret. She's a sweet girl and would never do something to hurt your feelings. You are such an amazing person, Maxie, so smart and kind. Your father and I know you are special, and *you* know you are special, and that's all that matters, right?"

She paused for a moment and flashed him a mischievous smile. "And I know for a fact that a certain Margaret Hart knows you are special, too."

"Aww, Mom," Max said. "You don't know that."

"Yes, I do, Maxie," his mother persisted. "You forget that Margaret's mother and I are very close friends and we like to talk about our children quite a lot, you know. I have heard more than once how Margaret thinks you are *such a sweet boy*."

"Aww, Mom…"

"Oh, and I almost forgot," she said, retrieving a piece of notebook paper from her apron pocket and handing it to Max. "Margaret's mother gave me this. She found it in the trash in Margaret's room."

Max carefully unfolded the crumpled paper. It was a drawing. Of him. Reading *The Hardy Boys*.

Max looked up at his mother.

"Margaret drew this?" he asked.

"Yes she did," his mother said, smiling.

"And…it was in the trash?"

"Well, Maxie, you did turn her down."

Oh yeah. I said no. I turned her down. Max was by no means a genius at understanding girls, but even *he* knew this much: maybe Margaret hadn't hated him before, but she certainly did now.

His mother, however, didn't seem to share the same train of thought. "Why, if I didn't know any better, Maxie," she said, "I'd think Margaret has a crush on you!"

"No she doesn't," Max responded automatically. After a moment's pause, however, he looked up from the drawing to meet his mother's eyes. "You think so? For reals?"

"Yes, for reals." His mother smiled. "She drew a picture of you, for goodness sake! I think you should go mend her broken heart.

Call her up right now and tell her you'll go to that dance with her. It would be a nice thing to do, Maxie."

"I don't know," Max said, fiddling with his shoelace. "Maybe I will…but you're sure she wasn't joking?"

"Yes, I'm sure! Now here's her phone number. I'll be in the kitchen making Sloppy Joe Sauce on Noodles."

Max sat there for a few minutes on his bedroom floor, back pressed up against the side of his bed, admiring Margaret's drawing of him. He cradled the phone in his lap and twirled the cord around his index finger, trying to muster up the few ounces of courage he possessed. Finally, he took a deep breath and dialed.

"Hello…um, may I please speak to Margaret?…Oh, this is Margaret? Hi, um, this is, um, this is Max—you know, Max Johnson?…Yeah, well I'm fine, thanks, how are you?…That's good. Um, yeah, well, I was calling because…because, um, well, I can go. To the dance. I can go to the dance with you. I mean, I would really like to go to the dance with you. That is, if you still want me to…You do? Great! I mean, you're not going with Timmy already?…Wait, really? You really turned Timmy down? Gee, that's super! I mean, okay, well I guess I'll see you tomorrow at school then…. Oh yeah—duh!—today' Friday. Well, I'll see you Monday then. Goodbye. Goodbye, Margaret."

*　　　*　　　*

Shuffle, shuffle, shuffle…

By now Max wasn't surprised to see Sean come running up to him when he came walking past the ball field, carrying his daily newspaper and a bag of groceries from the corner market. But today, the friendly boy was not wearing his usual smile.

"Hey, Mister! Can you call a doctor?" Sean hollered. "Mikey tripped in a crummy hole and hurt his ankle really bad!"

"Calm down," the old man said reassuringly. "Don't worry. Show me where Mikey is."

"Follow me," Sean said. "You know, Mini-Mikey's not much of a ballplayer, but he's still our friend."

*   *   *

"Ouch!" young Max grimaced, clutching his ankle and trying to stifle back tears.

"So, how did you say this happened?" Dr. Anderson asked, gently examining Max's left shin.

"Well, sir, I was walking home from the store with some flour for my mom—she was gonna bake me some chocolate chip cookies—and I guess I just wasn't paying attention…and well, sir, I tripped on a crummy crack in the sidewalk. The next thing I knew I was all sprawled out on the ground and covered in flour! Mom's gonna kill me."

"I guess that explains your new hairstyle," Dr. Anderson chuckled, referring to Max's white, flour-dusted head.

Max laughed in spite of himself, forgetting for a moment about his painful leg.

"Hmmm. Can you point your toes for me?" Dr. Anderson asked, applying slight resistance to the ball of Max's foot.

"Ouch! No, that hurts."

"Well, Max, I don't even need X-rays to tell you you've got yourself a pretty decent fracture here."

"What?"

"A broken leg, Max. I'll have to put a cast on it for four weeks, maybe six."

"Six weeks!?"

"I'm afraid so, but after that I promise it'll be good as new," Dr. Anderson said, beginning to wrap wet plaster around Max's injured leg.

"At least my mom can't make me play baseball for a while," Max quipped.

"Yes, running to first base on crutches might be a problem."

Max smiled. "Thanks for fixing me up, sir," he said.

"You don't have to thank me, Max. It is my job, after all."

At that moment, Max realized he wanted to be a doctor himself someday. Just like Dr. Anderson.

*   *   *

Max hurried as though he were twenty years younger to where Mikey was laying in the dirt near second base.

"Hello, son, I'm Max," he said to the teary-faced boy. "I'm going to take a look at his ankle of yours, okay? Don't worry. I promise everything's going to be fine." With a firm touch here and a gentle prod there, Max examined Mikey's swollen ankle.

"Can you point your toes for me?…Good. It's not broken, just sprained," Max assured the sniffling boy. The old man paused for a moment, then rummaged through his grocery bag. He pulled out a package of frozen broccoli.

"What's that?" Mikey asked.

"Broccoli, of course!" Max said with a grin. "Why, everyone knows broccoli heals sprained ankles."

"Yuck!" Mikey said, wrinkling his nose in disgust. "I hate broccoli!"

"Luckily, son, you don't have to eat it. It's frozen broccoli," Max explained, as he undid his necktie and used it to hold the package of broccoli in place on Mikey's injured ankle, "so it will work the same as an ice pack and help keep the swelling in your ankle down."

The boys looked on in awe.

"Now," Max continued, stroking his chin. "Be sure to put some...some frozen corn on it tonight, and...frozen cauliflower on it tomorrow!"

"Frozen corn and cauliflower?"

Max laughed. "Ice packs will work fine, too. In a couple days, you'll be good as new."

"Thanks, Mister," Mikey said appreciatively. "Without you walking by, I'd have been a gonner!"

"Oh, I doubt that."

"No, really, Mister, I'm glad you were around!" Mikey insisted. "Thanks for fixing me up."

"You don't have to thank me," Max said with a smile. "It is my job, after all."

"Do ya think he go see a doctor, Mr. Max?" Sean asked.

"He just did," Max said, smiling warmly and widely. "Well, a retired doctor, anyhow."

"Cool! So, will today be the day you play, *Doctor* Max?" Sean asked, still honestly hoping that the old man might say yes.

"Oh, no, no. I don't play baseball," Max answered.

"But I saw you make that great barehanded catch the other day! With a glove, you must be better than Derek Jeter."

"No, I don't think so," Max replied, laughing.

"Aww, please. Play just one game with us. You can be on my team," Sean pleaded.

You can be on my team. Max was shot back in time, back to that awful day when Timmy made the very same statement. *You can be on my team.* Max would not make the same mistake twice.

"Thanks, really, but I'd better get home before my wife Margaret starts to worry," Max said, and started to walk away. "She'll be wondering where her groceries are. As it is, I'll have to explain that I really *didn't* forget to buy broccoli!"

"C'mon, please!" Sean begged. "With Mikey hurt we're one man short now. We really need you to play. Just a couple innings. Why, I'll bet you can hit the ball as far as Barry Bonds—or even Babe Ruth!"

Max froze as still as a deer that's heard a twig snap. What he heard was his mom's words from so long ago: *Who knows, maybe you'll hit the ball as far as Bob Ruth!*

Max turned. "Oh, all right," he said with a hesitant smile. "You finally got me. I'll play, but just a few innings. And don't expect too much from me. I'm an old man, after all."

"Great!" Sean answered. "You can play center field."

"Nawww, you'd best stick me in right field," Max said, knowing full well his catch the other day was a mixture of pure luck and self-defense.

"Yeah, hide him in right field," interrupted Alex. "He's an old man, how good can he be? We're up by a run and only need three more outs. I don't want to blow this game!"

"You saw that catch he made the other day, Alex," Sean insisted. "He's a great player. Dr. Max is our new center fielder, and that's that!"

Max realized his anxiety must show on his face, because Sean laughed and gave him a pat on the back. "Just have fun. Play with your heart. You'll do great, Dr. Max! Here, wear my hat—it's in bad shape, but it's lucky," he said, placing his battered Chicago Cubs cap on the seventy-four-year-old rookie's bald head.

The lead was still one run, 12-11, with two outs in the final inning when…

…THWACK! The ball rocketed off the bat and headed towards the moon—and towards Max in center field.

Max backed up…backed up like Joltin' Joe DiMaggio…raised his glove and watched the leather comet come down and—YES!—

he felt the satisfying smack of the ball in the pocket of his glove. He couldn't believe it! He was the hero!

And then sixty years ago happened all over again. The ball popped out of Max's glove and fell to the ground and two runs scored. Max had not only lost the game again, he had lost his new friends. Now, as then, he dropped his borrowed glove and began to hurry away; away from all the eyes staring at him; away from Alex whining to Sean, "Why did you let the old man play? He lost the game for us! I knew he'd blow it!"

Then Max heard something else.

"Shut up, Alex!" Sean yelled, adding: "Hey Dr. Max! You'll come back and play again tomorrow, right?"

*   *   *

But Max did not come back the next day. Or the next. Or the day after that.

Sean figured his new old friend was embarrassed about losing the game and had started taking a different route for his daily walk. But on the fifth day of no Dr. Max, Sean decided to fix things.

"I don't know about you guys, but I miss having him around," Sean told his pals. "We've got to tell him we don't care that he dropped the ball. Let him know we want him to play some more. Whaddaya all say? Are you with me?"

The boys all nodded in agreement. All except one.

"Speak for yourself," Alex muttered.

*   *   *

KNOCK, KNOCK, KNOCK.

An elderly woman opened the door.

"Hi. I'm Sean. Me and the guys all play baseball down at the deserted lot on the corner. We're friends of Dr. Max. This is Mikey—Dr. Max fixed his ankle a few days ago. Anyway, we were wondering if we could talk to him for a minute. It's real important."

"Oh, you sweet dears. Please come in," Margaret said, sadly yet somehow sweetly. Fighting back tears, she continued:

"I'm afraid Max had a heart attack the other night...the night after he played baseball with you. He's...he's...Dr. Max is in heaven now."

Sean burst into tears.

"Don't cry. Please don't cry," Margaret whispered. "Max died as happy as I've seen him in all the time we were married, which would have been forty-eight years come next month. As happy as when he was accepted to medical school, even. Why, you should have seen the smile on his face the other day, beaming like the sun! He couldn't stop talking about you boys—especially you, Sean, about how you had kept asking him to play until he finally said yes. And how you didn't care he wasn't much of a baseball player—you made him feel welcome and were his friends, his real friends. He told me he couldn't wait to go back the next day to play another game with you boys."

By now the tears were streaming down Margaret's face, down every boy's face, even down Alex's freckled face.

"But how could he have been so happy?" Alex asked. "I mean, he did lose the game for us."

"Oh, sweetie," Margaret said. "You boys taught Max that it isn't just about winning and losing. It's about trying your best and having fun with your friends."

Margaret excused herself for a moment. She went to Max's den and came out holding a box with a dozen brand-new baseballs.

"Max wanted you boys to have these," she said, handing the box to Sean. "He said yours was pretty tattered and you could use some new ones. Oh, and Sean—he bought this for you," she added, handing him a brand-new Cubs ballcap.

*   *   *

The next morning, the boys were back at the vacant lot. But before picking teams, they made a sign and hung it on the fence: DR. MIGHTY MAX MEMORIAL FIELD.

Mikey's ankle was good as new, just as Dr. Max had promised, though his hitting and catching were as sickly as ever. With two outs and the game on the line, Mikey told Alex he should use a pinch hitter for him.

"You know I can't hit worth beans," Mikey said, his face pinched with worry. "I'll lose the game for us for sure."

"Naw, you just have to have a little faith in yourself," Alex said. "Grab a bat and remember to swing hard. You can do it...*Mighty Mikey!*"

Taking a deep breath, the littlest player then stepped to the plate and the brand-new baseball was pitched, and Mighty Mikey swung harder than he ever had before, and, miracle of miracles...

...THWACK!

All eyes watched the white, leather rocket soar higher and higher as though it were headed to the moon.

"Is it gonna be a home run?!" Sean shouted.

Alex smiled wisely: "Does it really matter?"

Lost and Found

Lily wasn't surprised anymore when she lost her voice. It happened all the time. Her voice was shy and small, often overpowered by her friends' snatches of gossip and loud shrieks of laughter. When Lily was called upon in class, her lips froze and her voice stubbornly refused to come out of her throat. It hid under the bed when her boyfriend Tad's kisses—and hands—became too aggressive.

Yes, Lily wasn't surprised anymore when she temporarily lost her voice. But one day, though she searched everywhere, she couldn't find it again.

Tad was the first to notice, although it took him four days. He sauntered over to Lily after his basketball game and asked what she thought of his spinning-one-handed-reverse-lay-up late in the third quarter. Lily just looked at him and smiled her quiet smile.

Tad's arrogant smirk quickly melted into angry disbelief. "Well, aren't you gonna say anything?" he demanded. Lily just smiled her quiet smile.

Tad said he was going out to Hudson's Grill with the guys to celebrate. He didn't invite Lily to join them. Two days later, he broke up with her for that perky cheerleader Charla with the peroxide-blonde hair and catty smile and chest as inflated as Tad's ego.

Tad told Lily it was because she didn't seem to really connect with him anymore.

"You understand, right, Babe?" he said, cracking his knuckles. Tad's hands reminded Lily of the disposable gloves she used last year when she dissected a frog in Biology. Rubbery and waxen, the fingers unnaturally swollen as if all the knuckles had been jammed during one of his basketball games. The boys in Lily's Biology class filled the rubber gloves with water until they were on the brink of bursting and then chased after the girls, threatening to drench their too-tight shirts and turn their freshly-straightened hair to frizz. Lily's hair was naturally straight, and all the girls told her she was *so lucky*. Lily didn't think so. They were the lucky ones, with their beautiful tousled curls. Straight hair was so dull and lifeless. But of course, Lily wasn't one to disagree. She just smiled her quiet smile and didn't say a word.

*   *   *

Even in their high school with a population of two-thousand, word spread as fast as e-mail spam. All it took was Tad and Charla walking to second period together, hand-in-hand, and before long it seemed everyone knew. Lily's friends swarmed around her like wasps, delirious with drama, screeching that "Tad is such a jerk!" and "Charla is such a slut!" and they can't believe Tad would do this to her when they had been together for "two whole months."

"Do you miss him something terrible?"

"Don't worry, we'll take you to the mall on Saturday and go shopping."

"That'll make you feel all better, won't it, Lil?"

The following Tuesday, there was a catfight in the girls bathroom because one girl had supposedly flirted with the other's boyfriend. By the time a teacher forced her way through the crowd of chanting students and into the bathroom, the flirt had a black eye, the accuser a bleeding lip, and all the toilets were flooded. Lily was old news and once again faded into the background. Her voice was still nowhere to be found.

When Lily arrived at school on Friday, her best friend Marianne was waiting for her by the rows of graffiti-tattooed lockers.

"Hi, Lil," Marianne said. "We need to talk. Did you get my note?"

Lily couldn't say anything, just raised her eyebrows quizzically.

Marianne sighed. "My note. I put it in your locker yesterday." She gestured at locker number 517 behind her.

Lily responded by opening her own locker, 518.

"Oh. Well, it doesn't matter," Marianne said, impatiently drumming her fingers against the locker's hard metal surface. "Lily, I've tried to be understanding. I mean, I know the whole Tad thing has been hard for you. But it's been two whole weeks. And the thing is, Lil, you've just…well, you've become depressing. You're no fun to be around."

Lily shouldered her blue backpack and turned to face her best friend. Marianne's favorite ice cream flavor was chocolate coffee swirl. Lily wondered if Marianne knew what *her* favorite ice cream flavor was.

"I just think we've grown apart, Lily," Marianne continued, the disdainful pity in her voice hastily disguised as an apology. "Sometimes these things just happen, you know? But I think it'd be best if we both moved on and went our separate ways. Okay?"

Lily watched her now ex-best friend strut away, a blur of blond highlights and a swishing green silk skirt, the jangling of her bracelets growing softer as Marianne disappeared amidst the crowd of students. Disappeared like Lily's voice.

Chocolate chip, Lily thought. *My favorite ice cream flavor is chocolate chip.* Lily closed locker number 518, slowly, carefully, so as not to make too much noise.

✳   ✳   ✳

After that, Lily began to spend her lunch hour in the library, silently eating her peanut-butter-and-banana sandwich in the company of Dickens, Hawthorne, and Thoreau. They did the talking and Lily did the listening, which worked out very well under the circumstances.

Lily did not see Marianne, or her other friends, much anymore. To Lily's surprise, she was okay without them. More than okay— she was filled with a sense of overwhelming relief. It was almost as if she had been waiting for The End, for an excuse to quietly slip out of her friends' lives into blissful obscurity. Lily still thought of Marianne fondly, and sometimes she even missed her, but it was in the same way she sometimes missed the old Disney Princess poster she had only recently gotten around to taking down off her bedroom wall. She didn't need it anymore, didn't relate to it anymore, didn't even really *like* it anymore, but she missed it simply because it had always been there, and now it wasn't.

✳   ✳   ✳

Wednesday. Two days gone and two more to go. Lily sat cross-legged on the carpeted floor, nestled against a bookshelf under one of the library's picture windows. She hoped to magically catch a ray of sunlight that could find the strength to break through the barricade of dark clouds suffocating the world. February was Lily's least favorite month. Enough time had passed to wear off the glittering hope of a new year, but the beginning of spring was not yet in sight.

Lily chewed her lunch absentmindedly, so enthralled in her latest book—*The Great Gatsby*—that she actually swallowed part of her granola bar's wrapper. Her English teacher was enchanted with the language of literature, exuberantly reading them passages from various works just to hear the texture and rhythm of the words. The rest of the class groaned, but Lily was secretly enamored. She had read *Gatsby* once before and found it good, but nothing special. Now it was like a whole new book; she could read into its soul. Her heart buzzed just to feel the weight of the words on her tongue.

> *The quiet lights in the houses were humming out into the darkness and there was a stir and bustle among the stars. Out of the corner of his eye Gatsby saw that the blocks of the sidewalk really formed a ladder and mounted to a secret place above the trees—he could climb to it, if he climbed alone, and once there he could suck on the pap of life, gulp down the incomparable milk of wonder...*

Lily felt as if she was Gatsby, climbing a ladder into the sky, to a place where she could listen to the music of the stars and tap-dance on the moon and never, ever have to come back to earth...

"Uh, excuse me?"

Lily started. She looked up into two enormous brown eyes. Kind eyes. They reminded her of the chocolate candies her grandmother made at Christmastime, before the chocolate hardened and they were just round pools of dark shining warmth.

"I'm sorry I startled you," the brown-eyed boy said. "I just need to get at a book behind you."

Lily scooted over. The boy crouched next to her, scanning the titles. He smelled clean, of soap and fresh laundry. Lily breathed in softly. Her heart felt suddenly warm, like it was wrapped in flannel sheets right out of the dryer.

He found the book he wanted and pulled it out triumphantly. Lily glanced over at the title. *The Grapes of Wrath.* A language treasure chest.

The boy caught Lily's glance and smiled. His smile was nice, starting with his eyes and slowly spreading across his face to reveal straight white teeth. Lily felt a thrill run down her spine, as if a secret had been unveiled before her eyes. She irrepressibly felt herself smile back.

"What are you reading there?" the boy asked, leaning closer to look at the book in her lap. "Ahh, Gatsby. One of my favorites."

Lily nodded. *Mine too,* she thought.

"My name's Jake, by the way," he added, reaching out to shake her hand. His eyes danced at her. Lily's soul tingled as his long fingers enclosed her own. *I'm Lily,* she thought, her voice still nowhere to be found.

Jake stood up. "Well, I'd better be going. It was nice meeting you."

You, too, Lily thought as she watched him walk away, trying to calm her racing heart. *Seems like a friendly guy. And what a smile! Too bad I'll probably never see him again.*

As Lily turned her attention back to *Gatsby,* she thought she caught a glimpse of her voice, peeking out from behind a curtain of thoughts swirling inside her. But it ducked away again, like a groundhog that has seen its shadow, disappearing in a fog of self-conscious doubt.

Despite Lily's hopes, the sun remained hidden as well, obscured by hazy gloom. Later that afternoon, the clouds started to rain and didn't pause to catch their breath for two whole days.

*   *   *

Lily leaned awkwardly against the library's front desk, sharpening a pencil. She liked to keep a little notebook beside her as she read so she could write down her favorite passages. She pulled her pencil out of the pencil sharpener and studied its tip. *Nope, still too dull.* She pushed it back in, careful to keep her fingers far away from the whirring machine.

When she was a little girl, Lily was scared of pencil sharpeners because she thought pencil-eating monsters lived inside. *What if one day the monster gets confused and gobbles up my fingers along with the pencil I'm sharpening? Fingers and pencils could look very similar to a monster, after all.* Now, of course, Lily knew better than to believe in monsters, but for some reason she never liked to sharpen a pencil until she absolutely had to, and when she did she kept her fingers at the very end, touching the eraser. Just in case.

Lily pulled her pencil out again. She smiled in satisfied relief. She wouldn't have to sharpen it again for awhile.

Notebook under arm, needle-sharp pencil in hand, Lily stepped quietly past shelves and shelves of books until she got to the very last row, then turned the corner and came into view of her special spot under the window…

…only to find it was already taken.

"Hi, there," he said. "I thought I might find you here." A single ray of sunlight streamed in through the picture window and fell across him, illuminating his face. Lily's breath caught in her throat.

He grinned sheepishly, holding up the open book Lily had left lying face-down on the floor while she went to sharpen her pencil. "Actually, this was a pretty good clue. I didn't think you would just leave *Gatsby* like that and never come back."

Lily smiled, at a loss for words. Of course, not knowing what to say was normal for her.

"I'm sorry," Jake said, breaking the silence and starting to get up. His eyes were so brown. "You obviously don't want me here, bugging you. I can find another spot."

No, it's okay. Lily went over and sat down beside him, pleading with her eyes to say what her voice couldn't. *Don't leave. It's nice to have company, sometimes.*

Jake seemed to read her thoughts—or maybe her eyes. He smiled. "You really don't mind if I stay? Okay. Cool." He sat back down, beside her, so close their knees touched. A shiver ran down Lily's spine. Part of her wanted to pull away, remembering the feel of Tad's waxen hands creeping across her skin. But then Jake reached over and handed *Gatsby* to her.

"Haven't you ever heard of bookmarks?" he teased. "Look at this delicate spine. You're going to break it, laying the book down open-faced like that. Better watch out. Before you know it, you'll be one of those heinous people who dog-ear the pages and I'll have to report you to the librarian!"

Lily rolled her eyes, teasing him back. His fingers brushed against hers as she took the book from him. Jake had nice, lean hands, strong but gentle. Not at all like Tad's.

She leaned back against the bookshelf and opened *Gatsby*, savoring the ray of winter sunlight warming her neck and falling across the page in front of her:

> *So he waited, listening for a moment longer to the tuning fork that had been struck upon a star...*

Lily wondered what that sounded like, a tuning fork being struck upon a star. Maybe it was something like the soft contented silence she shared with Jake at this moment, tranquility laced with energy that inflamed her, excited her, awoke her like a splash of ice-cold water, two different worlds quietly sitting together on the floor, linked by two gently-touching kneecaps.

*   *   *

Lily stretched out her legs and took a bite of her sandwich. Jake held out his mini-can of Pringles and Lily took a few, then offered him some sliced apples. He wrestled a slice out of the Ziploc bag and began eating it without taking his eyes off the open book in his lap. Lily smiled her quiet smile. She pretended to turn back to *Gatsby* but secretly watched Jake out of the corner of her eye, tracing his sturdy profile, the shaggy locks of dark hair falling gently across his forehead, his high cheekbones, his eyes intently jumping from word to word across the page in front of him. Jake got so into books it was as though his mind really traveled to a different place, a different time period, a different universe far, far away.

Oftentimes Jake didn't even hear the bell that signaled the end of lunch, and Lily had to gently tap him, *It's time to go*, until he looked up, his startled eyes meeting hers in momentary confusion, as if he had just woken up from a deep sleep. Then he would smile in an almost-embarrassed way, and gather up Lily's trash and stuff it into his brown paper lunch bag while she closed his book and put it in his backpack. He would stand up and reach down to help Lily up off the floor, and they would walk together out of the library and down the hall until they got to the sophomore lockers, where Lily would turn left to the English wing while Jake would say "See ya tomorrow!" and continue down the hall to Chemistry.

One day they walked by Lily's old friends who were gossiping outside the bathroom. The group of girls stopped mid-conversation to watch as Lily and Jake passed, not holding hands but walking close enough together that it was hard to discern whether they were a couple or not.

Marianne didn't care either way. In her mind, no guy was off-limits—except, of course, a geeky one. And Jake was definitely no geek.

"Hey, Lily!" she called, and ran to catch up with them. Lily paused, but Jake kept walking, and Lily realized: *He doesn't even know my name.* Somehow it had never really mattered before.

"Lily!!! How! Are! You!" Marianne didn't say it like a question. She was beside Lily now, gripping her arm like they were still best friends. Jake, meanwhile, realized Lily was no longer with him. He turned around and back-tracked, looking a bit confused to see Marianne, with her blonde highlights and twenty coats of mascara, standing beside Lily, who was still awkwardly clutching her notebook in her left hand.

"And who is *this*, Lil?" Marianne said, eyeing Jake and flashing her *Crest-with-Whitner* smile. "Aren't you gonna introduce us?"

Lily looked down at her shoes as the silence stretched from uncomfortable into unbearable. Finally Jake said, "Hi, I'm Jake."

"I'm Marianne. Lily's best friend."

No, she's not my friend. Not at all. Lily looked up, trying to meet Jake's eyes. *She's lying.* But Jake wasn't looking at Lily. "Wow, I had no idea you two were friends," he said.

"Oh yeah, the *best*," Marianne continued, twirling a strand of hair around her finger. "You must be new here. I know I would have noticed you before."

"Yeah. I just moved from Ohio, actually."

Lily sighed, looking back down at her mud-stained shoes. Stupid rain. Stupid dirty school. She knew the rest of this scene by heart. Jake would be won over by Marianne's flirty charm, just like the rest of the boys, and now he would walk with Marianne to class and forget all about quiet Lily. Everyone forgets about quiet Lily.

"Well, we'd better be going," Jake said. Lily looked up. "Nice meeting you, Marianne."

And then, to both Lily's and Marianne's utter astonishment, Jake touched Lily's arm and together they took off down the hallway.

"I'm sorry, if she's your friend," Jake said, "but I don't really care much for that Marianne girl. She seems so phony."

It was then Lily truly realized she didn't need Marianne anymore. She had found a new best friend.

Jake.

*   *   *

Lily usually avoided gossip like she avoided asparagus. But it was hard to ignore the rumors circulating the campus when she got to school on Monday. Tad and Charla had broken up. From what Lily could gather, it seemed Charla had cheated on Tad with a senior from Kentwood High.

"He's a football player who goes to our *rival school!* How much worse could it get?!" Marianne screeched to her entourage of giggling girls as Lily fiddled with her lock combination a few lockers away. "I heard Charla actually met the guy when she was cheering in the game last month against Kentwood. She thought he was hot, and got his number. Or something like that."

"Well, *I* heard the Kentwood guy didn't know she had a boyfriend, and he dumped Charla when he found out."

"Yeah, *I* heard that Tad actually saw them making out under the bleachers after one of Kentwood's games. Tad was with some of the football guys scouting for the next game. Or something."

"That sucks."

"Poor Tad."

Lily shut her locker. *Oh yeah. Poor, poor Tad.* She hoisted her backpack onto her shoulder and headed down the hall to the library.

Jake said yesterday he'd have a surprise for her today. She wondered what it could be.

*   *   *

Lily was early, or Jake was late. She sat down and read *Gatsby* while she waited for him. She was into the final chapter, and even though she knew how it ended, she still got breathless reading it. Final chapters are always the best. When Lily was in ninth grade she had a secret wish of reading the final chapter, if only the final chapter, of every single book in the entire school library. Now she was more realistic. She could live with only reading the final sentence. After all, if the final chapter is the whipped cream on the ice cream cone, the final sentence is the cherry on top.

Jake rushed in a few minutes later. He was half out of breath, as if he had been running, and he actually looked a bit disappointed to see her. But he quickly smiled, and Lily smiled back, and everything was all right. Just the sight of Jake made Lily's soul dance. She felt like a puppy, wagging its tail every time its favorite person comes nearby.

Jake sat down beside her. Lily looked at him. Waiting. *Okay, where's the surprise? Maybe he forgot.* Trying not to feel disappointed, Lily turned back to her book. She had only read a few sentences when Jake interrupted her. "How's the book coming?" he asked. Lily glanced over at him and shrugged. *Fine.*

"You're getting pretty close to the end, there, huh?"

Yep, she thought.

"Know what you're gonna read next?"

Lily shook her head. *Actually, I don't. I haven't really thought about it.*

"Oh."

Jake fell silent.

Why is he acting so strangely? Lily sighed and returned to her book.

"Hey, Lily?"

She glanced over at him, a bit annoyed. Her shrug implied: *What?*

"Could you, uh, go sharpen this pencil for me?"

Lily couldn't believe her ears. Of all the things to ask her to do! Sure, Jake didn't know she didn't like sharpening pencils. But still, why couldn't he just do it himself?

She gave him an exasperated glance, but made the mistake of looking into his eyes. "Please?" he said. Lily sighed and took the pencil from him. "Thanks!" he called after her as she disappeared around the corner of the aisle.

When Lily returned, after four fearful rounds of pushing the pencil into the sharpener for a few seconds and then pulling it out again to check its progress, Jake was writing on something in his lap. He looked up, saw her, and tried too late to hide it behind his back. "Uh, could you just, uh, go away for a minute?" he said with a sheepish grin. "I'm not done with your surprise yet."

Oh! So he didn't forget! Lily excitedly went into a nearby aisle and scanned the titles and titles of books, opening a few that intrigued her and reading their last sentences.

Salinger, J.D. *The Catcher in the Rye*. "Don't tell anybody anything. If you do, you start missing everybody."

Spinelli, Jerry. *Stargirl*. "Last month, one day before my birthday, I received a gift-wrapped package in the mail. It was a porcupine necktie."

Steinbeck, John. *Travels With Charley*. "And that's how the traveler came home again."

But Lily couldn't concentrate. Her heart was racing, yet it seemed less blood was reaching her brain. She could hardly think. A dozen or so final sentences later, she heard footsteps and Jake appeared. "Ready," he said. "Close your eyes." Lily obliged, and almost immediately felt the thrill of his warm hand in hers as he led her back to the spot—their spot—under the picture window.

"Okay," he said once they were settled on the floor. Lily opened her eyes to see Jake holding a present wrapped in tissue paper. "For you," he said with a grin.

Lily laughed in surprise. *What's this for?* she thought

"Go on, open it."

Lily ran her finger under the tape and carefully unwrapped the crinkly paper. She loved opening presents slowly, painstakingly slowly, to build the excitement.

It was…a book. A thick hardcover book. An expensive book. Lily turned it over. *The Grapes of Wrath.*

"I finished reading the library copy two nights ago," Jake said, leaning in closer. "I just had to get it for you. It's the best, Lil. My favorite book ever! I thought of you so many times when I was reading it—there are tons of passages you'll want to write down. I bet you'd fill up ten whole pages in your notebook before you even got half-way through. Seriously! So I got you your own copy, and now you can just write in the margins and underline right on the pages."

Lily smiled at him, running her fingers up and down the book's cover, feeling the smooth crisp newness of it. *Thank you. It's perfect. Absolutely perfect.*

"One of the main characters, Rose of Sharon, she reminds me a lot of you," Jake said. "She's quiet, but she's really strong, too. Inside, where it counts, you know? She's special." He was so close now Lily could count the freckles on his nose. "Like you."

Special. I'm special? It sounded nice. *Special.* Lily couldn't remember anyone ever using that word to describe her before.

She liked it.

"Oh, and I have something else." Jake pulled out a skinny flat rectangle folded in a single sheet of tissue paper. "It's not much, but…"

Lily unwrapped it, fingers trembling slightly.

"It's a bookmark. So now you won't have to worry about cracking some poor book's spine or—God forbid—dog-earing its pages!"

On one side, Jake had drawn a picture of Lily, smiling her quiet mysterious smile, as if she knows a wonderful secret. Lily turned the bookmark over. Jake had written a passage on the other side.

"That's what I was doing just now," he said. "I had to look it up in your notebook. I wanted to get it exactly right."

It was from *Gatsby*. Lily had read these words so many times she practically knew them by heart.

> *His heart beat faster and faster as Daisy's white face came up to his own. He knew that when he kissed this girl, and forever wed his unutterable visions to her perishable breath, his mind would never romp again like the mind of God…. At his lips' touch she blossomed for him like a flower and the incarnation was complete.*

Lily felt warm tears running down her cheeks. She didn't even know why she was crying, but she was, and it felt good. This was her favorite passage in the entire book, the part when Gatsby realizes he truly loves Daisy.

"What's wrong? Don't you like it?" Jake asked, and Lily smiled, *Oh, yes, it's perfect, absolutely perfect*, and then she was laughing, too, and she didn't even know why. Jake leaned in and brushed the tears from her cheeks with his soft hands. Lily closed her eyes, trying to memorize the moment, and then suddenly she felt Jake's lips touch her own. For a split second she thought of Tad and wanted to pull away, but Jake was gentle and kind and his hands were warm and tender on her face, and so she breathed in his wonderful clean scent and kissed him back. *At his lips' touch she blossomed for him like a flower and the incarnation was complete.* Lily's heart opened wide, so wide she could gaze inside it, and in astonishment she saw her voice, her shy little beautiful voice, sitting there smiling in a knowing way, as if it had been waiting for her.

Hi, Lily, it said. *What took you so long?*

*   *   *

Lily stood at locker 518, trying to decide which books she needed for homework. It was Friday. Lily loved Fridays, especially Fridays in April. The weather was supposed to be nice this weekend, sunny and warm. Jake was going to take her on a picnic at the beach. He was fascinated with the beach. He said when you've lived all your life in a place like Ohio, the ocean seems new and miraculous and you want to visit it every chance you get.

Someone came up from behind and Lily turned, smiling, her lips tingling with expected kisses, but to her surprise Tad, not Jake, was standing before her. He was smiling, only it wasn't a nice smile; it was fake, like Marianne's. It made Lily shiver.

"Hey, Lil," he said. "How's it goin', Babe?"

I'm not your babe. Lily shoved books into her backpack furiously. Math, Spanish, Chemistry. *What else, what else? Is that all I need?*

"So, ya miss me? I've missed you."

Yeah, right, she thought.

"Listen, Lily, I've been thinking…" Tad leaned in towards her, bringing his face close to hers. His breath smelled like Altoids. Lily fought the urge to gag. She hated Altoids. They were so strong, so overpowering—just too much, in her opinion. Of course, she'd never actually told anyone that. Everyone else at her school was practically addicted to Altoids.

"Lily, I made a big mistake. I never should have broken up with you. It was just a really confusing time in my life, Babe, and I didn't really know what I wanted. Ya know? But now I realize…"

Tad hadn't shaved all week, and there was some stubble on his chin, like tiny flecks of dirt. There was a time when Lily thought he was the cutest guy she had ever laid eyes upon. She remembered how her knees literally buckled when he asked her to the movies that first time. But now, he seemed disgusting. So hopeless and immature and vain…she almost felt sorry for him.

"…I realize you're the one for me, Babe. Charla was just—one of those things, ya know? But I never really had any feelings for her. Not like with you. You're the chick for me, Lily. You're special."

Special. The word was poison coming from his repulsive mouth. Tad's rubbery-lab-glove hands grabbed her wrists, and he leaned in, pressing her against the hard metal lockers as his face grew closer and closer…

"NO!"

Lily felt the word escape, like a caged bird frantically beating its wings harder and harder against the metal bars until it finally breaks free and soars off into the sky.

"NO! No, no, no, NO! No, Tad. Get off me!" Lily twisted away from his grasp, panting with anger and fear and frustration and unabashed jubilation. Her voice was back! She had found it, and she had used it, and she was free.

A few people chatting in groups nearby noticed the commotion and turned to look. Tad ran his pudgy fingers through his oily hair and glared at her. "Okay, already, just calm down." He turned around slowly and sauntered away, his huge boots crunching on the gravelly dirt.

Lily watched Tad leave, enjoying a sweet sense of triumph. Then she slammed her locker door shut, hard, and hurried off to the library.

*   *   *

He was sitting there, reading, just as she had hoped. When he saw her he smiled and his brown eyes lit up.

"Hi, Jake," Lily said, and her voice sounded strong and sure. "You won't believe how much I have to tell you."

The Hitchiker

Jessica Sanbreiner drove up the Southern California coast on the 101 Freeway, talking sixty-miles-an-hour on her cell phone while driving seventy-five—and still getting passed. Suddenly, something caught her eye in the rear-view mirror. Something *inside* her SUV. Darkened by shadows, it moved closer. Jess felt the hair on the back of her neck stand at attention.

She shrieked.

"Jess, what is it?" her friend's worried voice crackled across the statticky cell-phone connection. "Are you okay?"

"Yolanda, hold…" Another shriek. "STOP! Stop right where you are! Don't come any closer!"

But the shadowy figure crept slowly towards her, and Yolanda, a hundred miles away, could do nothing but listen helplessly to her friend's terrified pleas.

*   *   *

When Jessica first told them her vacation plans, her three best friends all said they were in. A road trip up the California coast, snapshots at a handful of quaint tourist shops and vineyards along the way, culminating in a visit to the National Steinbeck Center and a tour through the great author's hometown of Salinas.

Okay, so maybe it wasn't what most people would pick as their dream vacation destination. But Jess had long been an ardent John Steinbeck fan—and not just because they shared the same initials. She still vividly remembered the first book of his she read: *The Grapes of Wrath*. At thirteen, she had never before tackled a book so thick, but she finished it within a few days and loved it so much she promptly read the whole thing again, cover to cover. There was something about the seemingly effortless way Steinbeck wove a story together: his perfectly chosen words, his detailed descriptions, his characters so painfully honest that it made Jess's very soul ache with recognition. Indeed, it was Steinbeck's work that inspired Jess to want to become a writer herself someday.

That "someday" had arrived. Now she was twenty-six years old, the author of two modestly reviewed, semi-decent-selling novels. And yet neither book brought her great pride, deep satisfaction—or much money, for that matter. Jess had started her latest novel attempt two months earlier and already she could feel it dying, the life being slowly sucked away by too many one-dimensional characters, clichéd similes, and overly dramatic dialogue. She needed something to inspire her, to get her writer's blood pumping, to give her creativity the kick in the culottes it so desperately needed. Steinbeck's hometown, she hoped, would be the magic elixir. Maybe she could absorb some of his genius through osmosis.

And so the road trip was on.

Then it was off.

The problem? A passenger. Or, rather, a lack thereof.

At first her friends had marveled at the plan's utter brilliance, but by the time June rolled around and Jess needed a commitment, a whirlwind of urgent "more important" business came up. Cindy had a wedding to attend. Tina was going camping with her Boy-friend-of-the-Month.

Even Yolanda, Jess's best friend, backed out. "You know how busy it is right now at the restaurant, Jess," she explained. What a lame excuse! Yolanda worked at Wendy's, but she insisted on referring to it as *the restaurant*. "My boss would kill me if he found out I took a week off to travel to some museum."

Some museum! Jess fumed and declared that if Yolanda really felt that way about Steinbeck—that his beloved Salinas was just "some museum"—she didn't want her to come anyway. She would have a grand time on her own, thank-you-very-much.

Despite backing out on the trip, Yolanda made Jess promise to call every once in awhile to check in. "Just to be safe," Yolanda said. "I want to make sure your car doesn't break down, you aren't wandering the roads completely lost, and you haven't picked up a murderer-slash-rapist disguised as a handsome hitchhiker."

Of course, Yolanda was just joking about the latter—"Really, Jess, you'd never be so dumb as to take on a hitchhiker when you're alone, even if he looks like Brad Pitt, right?" But now, listening to her friend's shrieks over the phone, it seemed the worst-case-scenario was actually coming true. Jess had always harbored a weakness for cute guys.

*   *   *

"Where are you, Jess? Did you hit something? Talk to me!"

"No, Yolanda, I'm…Hold it right there, Buster. Don't come any closer!" The intruder was in plain sight now, close enough to strike. Time for desperate measures.

Still clutching the cell phone in her right hand, Jess used her right knee to hold the steering wheel straight, reached down with her left hand and yanked off one of her imitation Doc Martens—

"Intern Martens," she called them—and fiercely began swinging the fashionably clunky shoe at the intruder while trying not to swerve off the road. Suddenly a siren wailed, and red and blue lights flashed in her rearview mirror.

A wave of relief washed over Jess. "Gotta go, Yolanda. I'll call you back soon, 'k?" she said, ignoring her friend's protests and flipping the phone closed. Jess smiled smugly at her unwanted passenger. "You're gonna get it now!" she hissed.

Yolanda tried calling back, but there was no answer.

*   *   *

Jess's trip had started out rather unremarkably. She managed to make it out of Manhattan Beach without hitting much traffic and smoothly headed north up the Pacific Coast Highway. She stopped near Oxnard to help a high-school-aged guy with shaggy hair and bad acne change a flat tire. Jess had helped like this numerous times, and people were always stunned that "such a nice young woman" could change a tire. Jess always explained that she had taken auto shop in high school, after her then-boyfriend said, only half-jokingly, that "girls are meant to change diapers, not tires." Of course, Jess proved him wrong.

Jess planned to stop in Oxnard anyway, because her friend Cindy swore they grew "The World's Best Strawberries" there. Then she headed off again, singing out-loud (and off-key) to Lee Ann Rimes and reaching back every few miles to grab a handful of strawberries from the carton in the backseat. *Hey, Cindy's right, these really are The World's Best!*

It wasn't until she passed through Santa Barbara nearly forty-five minutes later and called Yolanda to check in that Jess glanced in the rear-view mirror and caught a glimpse of her intruder. He must have snuck in at the strawberry stand.

*   *   *

Well, now he's gonna get what he deserves! Jess thought, pulling her Jeep Grand Cherokee over to the shoulder of the freeway. She rolled down her window. "My God, I'm happy to see you!" she said when the CHP officer strolled up to her driver's door.

The officer looked slightly puzzled. He wasn't the least bit amused. "License and registration, please," he ordered matter-of-factly.

"What? Oh, no, you don't understand—"

"License and registration," he repeated. "How many drinks have you had today, Ma'am?"

"None. I haven't been drinking. Just bottled water, I mean. I can explain—"

"What I would like you to explain," the officer interjected sternly, "is why you were weaving recklessly while going fifteen miles-per-hour above the speed limit, talking on a cell phone and…" He eyed the Doc Marten knock-off in Jess's hand. "…and putting on your shoes?"

"Oh, I wasn't putting my shoe on."

"No?"

"I was taking it off. You see, there's an intruder in my car and I was trying to smack him with it."

"Uh-huh." The officer's all-business expression grew even more serious. With his hand on his holstered gun, he surveyed the interior of the Jeep. "Well, it looks like he's not here anymore, so if you could please get out your license…"

"He's right over…" Jess glanced to her right. "Wait, he disappeared. That tricky devil! I know he's still here somewhere."

The officer opened the rear doors and checked the floor. Then he looked in the back under Jess's travel bags. By now he was really not amused. "Ma'am, I can assure you, there is no man in your car."

"Oh, I know that."

"Excuse me?"

"I wasn't talking about a man. The intruder is a…spider."

"Spider?"

"Yes! A big, hairy one. Snakes don't bother me, you know, but spiders really give me the creeps! This one somehow snuck into my car and was crawling along the top of the passenger's headrest and it kept coming closer and closer—"

"Ma'am, please step out of the vehicle."

Fifteen minutes later, after even more explaining, a breathalizer test that proved she wasn't drunk, and a promise to never again attempt to take her shoe off while driving, the officer finally let Jess go—with a two-hundred-and-seventy-dollar speeding ticket.

She was not back on the road five full minutes before her intruder reappeared, making its way across the dashboard on the passenger side. True to her promise, this time Jess pulled the Jeep over and stopped before taking her shoe off.

"You little bugger!" she sneered, "Intern Marten" in hand, as she leaned in for the kill. "I'm going to squash you like a bug, you bug, and then I'm going to mail you in along with the two-hun-dred-and-seventy bucks for this damned speeding ticket!"

Just then the Jeep was filled with the "I Hope You Dance" ring-tone of Jess's cell phone. Keeping a wary eye on the spider, she reached down and picked the phone up from the floor where she had flung it. "Hello?"

"Jess, is that you?!" Yolanda sounded close to tears. "I was so worried! What the hell happened?"

"Let's just say I had an unwanted visitor." Jess proceeded to tell her friend about the hitchhiking spider, the shoe incident, the ill-mannered CHP officer, and the two-hundred-and-seventy dollars she now owed Governor Schwarzenegger.

Yolanda was furious. "Jess, I can't believe you! All that for a little *spider*? The way you were screaming, I thought you were being attacked by Freddy Kroger."

"*Kruger*, Yolanda. Freddy *Kruger*. If you're gonna bring up the King of Horror, make sure you get his name right. Anyway, you should see this spider. It's the size of your purse, for God's sake."

"Whatever, Jess. For a horror movie psycho, I'd say you're pretty chicken. Why don't you just admit it so I can get back to work?"

"I'm *not* chicken! You'd have been scared, too, Yolanda. Fake Hollywood gore is one thing. Big, hairy, real-life spiders are quite a different matter. This really is an eight-legged freak!"

"You couldn't survive one day with that spider in your car."

"Could too!" Jess wished she could smack her friend with her shoe right about now. Yolanda sounded just like Jess's stupid ex-boyfriend. "I could survive the whole trip with a spider in my car if I wanted to."

"Oh yeah? I dare you."

"You're on."

"Loser buys lunch."

"Okay."

"It's a bet," Yolanda agreed. "Well, I'd better get back to work. The restaurant is pretty busy today. I'm just glad you're all right, Jess. I was worried, but I can see you're back to your regular delusional self. Toodle-loo."

Jess opened her mouth to deliver a sharp retort, but Yolanda had already hung up. Still clutching her shoe, Jess looked around for the spider, but once again it was nowhere to be seen. Her heart jumped for a moment as she imagined it crawling along the back of her headrest, but then she shook her head and calmed herself. Maybe, if she was lucky, it fell down the air vent and she wouldn't have to deal with it anymore.

Two Lee Ann Rimes CDs and enough strawberries to turn her lips Maybelline glossy red later, Jess pulled up to the Oceanside Bed & Breakfast in Cambria. It was early evening and the sun was just setting. Despite the CHP incident, she had made good time.

Still no sign of that blasted spider. *Good riddance*, Jess thought, but she left out a few strawberries on the dashboard, just in case it was hiding somewhere between the seat-cushions and got hungry during the night. If it reappeared, she had to keep it alive until the end of the week, so she could show Yolanda. Then, once the bet was won, Jess would waste no time in smashing it with the clunky heel of her shoe.

*   *   *

Cindy was dead-on about those Oxnard strawberries. The World's Best. Even the spider seemed to like them, for upon climbing into her Jeep the next morning, Jess discovered it was back. And it had spun a web. In her car. Next to the strawberries she left out.

There it sat—if spiders can sit—suspended by silk threads, in the corner where the car roof slopes down to meet the dashboard. At least it was cordial enough to stay over on the passenger side.

Jess's first thought was to tear the web down. But she resisted the urge because: one, she had to prove Yolanda wrong; and two, she didn't want to get any closer to the spider than she had to. Maybe if she stayed on her side of the car, it would stay in its little web and leave her alone.

"Hey buddy, just to let you know," Jess said as she rocketed out of the parking lot, "that contraption of yours won't work too well in here. There aren't many bugs crawling around in a car. I mean, I've had a few flies before, but they always escape out the window the first chance they get. You're the first creature who's ever cared to stay, come to think of it. Heck, even my boyfriends don't usually stick around too long."

Jess glanced over at the hitchhiking spider. It was sitting very still in its web—*sleeping?* she wondered. *Do spiders even sleep?* Or perhaps it was plotting an attack. Maybe the next time she got out of the Jeep at a gas station, she'd come back to find it perched atop her headrest, ready to bite her with deadly poison that would leave her paralyzed in a matter of minutes…or at least cause a gross, itchy rash.

"You know, you don't have to stay here for me," Jess said. "You can scuttle out of here the first chance you get. I won't be offended, I promise."

But the spider seemed perfectly content where it was, and, aside from conducting a double-check search of the driver's seat before climbing in after a restroom stop, Jess wasn't much of a mind to bother it.

"So, we're gonna be spending a lot of time together the next few days," she said eighty miles (and sixty minutes) later, glancing over at the eight-legged hitchhiker. Jess didn't know much about spiders, so she wasn't sure what type it was. Not a black widow, she hoped.

"I should probably introduce myself. My name is Jessica Sanbreiner, but you can call me Jess. Everyone does. Well, I guess I should give you a name, too. Hmmm…what's a good name for a spider? Charlotte? No, that's already taken. Besides, you seem like a guy spider, for some reason. Spider-Man? Spidey? No, too Hollywood. I'll think of something.

"Anyway, you're probably wondering about that crazy woman on the phone? That's my friend, Yolanda. She thinks I won't be able to restrain myself from squishing you or flicking you out the window. But don't worry, I have an unbelievable amount of self-control. Those strawberries yesterday were an exception to the norm. Hey, stop laughing.

"What I do for a living? Well, thanks for asking. I'm a writer. I know, pretty cool, huh? The only problem is I'm having trouble with my latest manuscript. What kind of trouble? Well, it's hard to explain. The story just isn't working for me. It's dying. Steinbeck would roll over in his grave if he read it. Or he'd take away my laptop. Heck, maybe someone *should* take my computer away. Give it to somebody who can actually use it. It's not like the contraption's been much help to me lately.

"What? Why don't I stop whining and start writing? Listen, buddy, it's not that easy. You non-writers just don't understand what it's like. It's grueling work, for your information! Grueling!

"Anyway, I'm headed to the Steinbeck Museum in Salinas because I'm hoping it will help get me back on track. Have you ever read Steinbeck? No? Never?! Oh, you poor deprived soul! He's the best. Maybe the museum will have some books on tape that we can listen to on the drive home. What's my favorite book of his? Oh, that's a tough one. That's like asking me to choose between Ben & Jerry's Chunky Monkey and their Chocolate Chip Cookie Dough. Hmmm. I guess I'd have to say my first love is *The Grapes of Wrath*, but I just finished reading *Travels With Charley* again and that is an awfully good piece of literature, too. What's it about? Well, you see, Steinbeck goes on this trip with his dog, Charley, and…

"Wait a minute. That's it! I know what your name should be. Charley! Get it? This trip can be *my* Travels With Charley. It's quite brilliant, if I do say so myself. Don't you think?"

Charley remained suspended in his web, as though he were in a silk hammock, motionless except for the gentle rocking movement of the Jeep. *I wonder if he's carsick*, Jess thought. *Or maybe he's hungry*. He hadn't taken a bite out of the strawberries she had left him.

Okay, so spiders don't care for strawberries, even if they are The World's Best. Hmmm, what do spiders eat then, besides insects?

Jess was getting pretty hungry herself, come to think of it. She got off the next exit and pulled over to the first place she glimpsed that wasn't a McDonald's, Taco Bell, or Wendy's *restaurant*. A faded sign proclaimed "Big Billy's Burgers: The Best in Town!" and from the vast array of big rigs crowding the parking lot, Jess guessed it must be a popular hangout for truckers. Her dad always proclaimed truck drivers had a sixth sense for "good grub." She hoped he was right.

"Behave yourself, Charley, I'll be back soon!" Jess said, opening her door. "I'll try to bring you some crackers or something. You like crackers? Or maybe a packet of ketchup? Spiders like tomatoes, after all. Think of ketchup as fast-food tomatoes."

*   *   *

Big Billy's was a highway-town cliche. Red vinyl booths, white-and-black checkerboard tile floor, tired waitresses wiping down grimy Formica tables with rags so dirty they were just making matters worse.

A young couple sat together on the same side of one of the booths. Across the room, a weary mother tried to coax her toddler to eat a few more bites of a grilled cheese sandwich, but he seemed more interested in playing with the salt and pepper shakers. The only other customers were four burly men enjoying "Big Billy's Burger Special" at the counter.

Jess sat down at one of the booths and ordered a Big Billy's Burger with a bowl of tomato soup substituted for the greasy French fries.

The soup came. There were alphabet letters floating in it like tiny odd-shaped boats. Jess noticed one "boat" was curiously dark-hued.

"Excuse me, Miss?" Jess said, flagging down the nearest waitress—"Glenda," according to her Big Billy's nametag. "This sounds like a bad joke, but I swear I'm not kidding. There truly is a fly in my soup."

"Well, look at that. I reckon you want another bowl," the waitress said without a hint of apology. She reached in to sweep the bowl away.

"Hold it," Jess stopped her. "New soup would be great, but do you think you could get me a little container to keep that fly in?" Glenda looked at her as if she had asked for a Big Billy's Lobster Tail. "It's, uh, it's for a science experiment…" The waitress still appeared doubtful, but she compliantly brought back the fly in a glass jelly jar along with a fresh bowl of soup.

Upon returning to the car, Jess tentatively set the tomato-soup-drowned fly on the outskirts of Charley's web. "Here ya go, bud," she said, then promptly forgot about it in her concentration to get back on the freeway. By the time she glanced over at Charley nearly half an hour later, the fly was gone. She hoped it was inside her passenger's stomach and hadn't just fallen to the floor.

* * *

The museum was impressive. No, it was more than that. To Jess, Steinbeck was not merely a brilliant author; he was practically a god. And this museum, at the head of Main Street in Salinas' Historic Old Town, was his chrome-and-glass temple. Jess was suddenly nervous. She felt like she had stumbled upon the threshold of a sacred place, and she wasn't quite sure how to act.

Oh, if only Yolanda had come along! Jess thought. *I can't go in there alone.* Glancing over at her web-spinning companion, Jess weighed her options. She could venture in by herself. Or…

"Hey, Charley, you want to come with me, don't you?" Jess found the glass jelly jar the waitress had given her as a fly "doggie bag" and poked some holes in the lid with a ballpoint pen. She held the open jar on its side on the dashboard, gently prodding the spider towards it with the tip of the pen. "C'mon, Charley, it'll be fun. You haven't come all this way just to chicken out at the very end, have you?" Eventually Jess was able to maneuver the spider into his makeshift traveling carriage. She screwed on the lid and tucked the jar into the mini-backpack she used as a purse.

The two traveling companions spent nearly four hours exploring the museum. Jess kept a notebook in her back pocket and scribbled down notes and descriptions of most everything she saw. Her favorite quote was from one of Steinbeck's journals: "I nearly always write, just as I nearly always breathe." Jess breathed in deeply, filling her lungs with museum air, hoping some of the magic would enter her bloodstream. "Steinbeck's right, Charley," she whispered. "Writing isn't just a career. It's a way of life."

The writer and the hitchhiker saw a video about Steinbeck's childhood, exhibits about his various works, a gallery of photographs inspired by *The Grapes of Wrath*. There were pictures of Steinbeck and his family, simulations of the workers' bunkhouse from *Of Mice and Men* and Doc's workshop from *Cannery Row*, and—Jess's favorite—Steinbeck's actual green pickup-camper "Rocinante" in which he traveled across America with his Charley.

"It's smaller than I expected. Don't you think, Charley?" Jess said, slowly circling it, enchanted, like a child surveying a very large Christmas present and trying to guess what treasure lies inside. A few visitors looked at her strangely, no doubt assuming she was talking to the life-sized plastic model of Steinbeck's dog perched in the front seat of the camper.

Their last stop was the extensive Steinbeck gift shop. Jess bought a T-shirt and seven of Steinbeck's books on tape—"I would buy you some of this Steinbeck candy, Charley, but you're such a picky eater!" she laughed. She did find a pill bug in the parking lot, though, and that seemed to suffice.

Later that night, in her room at the Salinas Good Nite Inn, Jess pulled out her iMac laptop and started working on her manuscript. Just as she hoped, the visit to Steinbeck's museum had rejuvenated her creativity. Or perhaps it was not so much the final destination that had inspired her as the road trip there, because she found herself writing about—of all things—Charley.

Spiders, I've discovered, are marvelous travel companions. They don't complain or get carsick. They don't argue with you about which CD to listen to. They don't need restroom stops every twenty minutes. They don't like to eat strawberries or chocolate, which means more of both for you! While they may seem like picky eaters, the truth is your everyday fly or pill bug will satisfy them just fine.

I used to be afraid of spiders. Terrified, actually, with a capital T. But then Charley, my very own eight-legged friend, entered my life through a carton of strawberries and taught me that you can find companionship in the most unlikely of places...

Before she knew it Jess was typing furiously, the words and ideas coming as fast as her fingers could dance on the keyboard. She wrote and wrote and wrote long into the night.

*　　　*　　　*

"Okay, you win," Yolanda admitted when Jess called her upon returning home to Manhattan Beach. "I still can't believe you kept that spider the whole trip. I guess I underestimated your stubbornness."

"I'm *not* stubborn!" Jess said, plopping down on the couch, feeling weary yet wonderful at the same time. She kicked off her Intern Martins, first the right one—*thud!*—and then the left—*clunk!* "But anyway, I'm kind of worried," she continued. "I don't know where Charley went. He wasn't in his web when we got home, and I searched all through the Jeep but I couldn't find him."

"He probably just disappeared into a crack in the seat cushion," Yolanda said. "I'm sure he'll show up."

"Yeah, you're probably right. He'll show…oh, NOOOO!" Jess screamed. Her left shoe had knocked over her glass of iced tea and spilled it all over the white carpet. And on the bottom of the sole was the unmistakable flattened form of a squashed hitchhiker.

JUST FRIENDS

He stares straight ahead, face awash in the dim red glare of the stop-light. He taps out a melody on the steering wheel with his thumbs. He is beautiful.

"Do you love her?" I ask suddenly, squeezing the foam Disney-land heart, *Be Mine* embossed in script across its surface like some second-grade Valentine.

His eyes meet mine, briefly. "Yes," he says, and it is something simple, definite, a math equation with the same answer every time. *Is two-plus-two four? Yes.* Easy as that.

It is the meanest thing he's ever said to me.

The light turns green and he takes me home.

*   *   *

I have this plant on my desk in a small clay pot. A real plant, with real soil. I water it every Tuesday. My aunt gave it to me for my sev-enteenth birthday. "It's good for your *chi*," she explained, her pen-ciled-on eyebrows drawn together in seriousness.

I don't know about *chi*. I don't even know what kind of plant this is. I think it's some sort of flower, but I'm not sure. There aren't any blooms on it right now.

*   *   *

Sometimes I lie awake at night and stare at my ceiling. At first it's kind of boring, but after awhile you start to see things. Images, pictures, like movies unwinding above your head. Sometimes I don't understand what they mean, and sometimes they don't seem to make sense—dancing bears changing into a flock of flying birds changing into me, naked, standing in the kitchen of some house I've never been to. I used to think maybe they were predictions of the future, but not one has come true yet.

I don't try to wish meaning into things anymore. It's too depressing.

You have to keep staring, and staring, because if you blink the images disappear and your ceiling is just a regular ceiling again, flecks of white paint peeling off in places. You have to keep staring, because when you do it's almost like you're dreaming, but your eyes are open. Sometimes I wonder if that's what it feels like to die. And sometimes I think no, that's what it feels like to live.

*   *   *

"This'll probably sound stupid," he says.

I don't say anything, just raise my eyebrows a bit, chewing my gum. I usually don't like to chew gum. It makes me feel like a cow chewing her cud. But he gave me the gum, so I chew it and almost forget that I don't like it.

"So yesterday I was driving around," he continues, just as I knew he would, without any response from me, "and I suddenly felt like—I don't know, it's hard to explain—like maybe I wasn't really *here*, you know? Like what if I don't exist at all? What if it's all in my head?"

We're parked at Surfer's Point, looking out at the midnight waves. A palm tree sways slightly in the April breeze.

"No," I say. "That's not stupid at all."

Later, he drives me home. The Beatles sing "Let It Be" and the stars are bright and the dashboard is dusty. He smells like vanilla, which would be weird on anyone else but is perfect on him. He doesn't try to kiss me goodnight. It doesn't come as a surprise but hurts nonetheless. I feel how ice cubes must feel, clinking against each other, trapped inside a glass.

I spit out the gum in my bathroom sink. I look at it for a moment, and then I change into an oversized T-shirt and climb into bed and lie with my legs under the sheet but not the covers because even though it's still a little chilly out I've never cared much for layers of insulation. Too restricting. My bedroom window is open a couple of inches and I know I will wake up in a few hours, curled into the fetal position, trying to get warm. I will give in and pull the covers up from their rumpled post at the foot of my bed. But for now, the thin sheet is enough.

I try to stare at the ceiling but it doesn't work, not tonight.

In the morning the gum is a hard round blob. I pick it off the porcelain and throw it in my trash can but there is still a tiny film of gum residue left inside the sink. You wouldn't notice it, if you didn't know it was there. But I know it is there and this makes me sad, for some reason. I wish I wasn't so reckless.

*   *   *

When I was six I wanted an invisible friend. All my real friends also had invisible friends. I wanted one too.

So. I tried making one up. A girl, like me. In first grade, like me. Red hair, brown eyes, a mole on her left cheek below the jawline.

Her name was Molly Hudson. I don't know why I chose the name Molly Hudson. It sounded nice, I guess.

The first day we decided to play tea party. Actually, I decided, and Molly didn't object. I carefully placed the teacups on their paper doilies, the plastic crumpets on their plastic plates, the teapot a queen bee in the center of the table. Then we sat down.

It only lasted a few minutes. I tried talking to Molly, but she never responded. I tried smiling at her, but she never smiled back. I tried, but I could never quite see her, sitting across the table from me. I felt stupid.

So my invisible friend—who never appeared—disappeared. I lost her. I guess, even at six years old, I didn't have enough imagination. A few weeks later, I thought I caught a glimpse of Molly Hudson, a flash of red hair and serious brown eyes, but then I realized I was looking into a mirror.

*   *   *

My mother comes with me to pick out my graduation announcements. I tell her I can go by myself, but I think she's afraid I'll pick out the wrong ones. I probably would.

She is upset because we have to buy our caps and gowns instead of renting them. "That's the most ridiculous thing I've ever heard!" she says, like it is a personal affront to her parenting skills. I tell her maybe I can borrow Jenny's cap and gown. Jenny is my cousin. She graduated last year. But my mother will have none of it. She prefers to argue.

I pick out the simplest design for my announcements: plain namecards, block lettering, the minimal amount of gilded swirls around the border. My mother favors the more ornate ones, with the formal sticker seals and gold embossing. We end up getting those.

*   *   *

"Of course we'll stay in touch," he says.

I lean back against the headrest and close my eyes. I have a headache. I try to picture writing him e-mails and I can't. I try to picture college and I can't envision that either.

"Yeah," I say. "I know we will."

*   *   *

For Christmas my mother got my dad a silk shirt with Hawaiian print. He didn't like it but pretended he did, trying it on and modeling it for us with a too-tight smile. "Thank you," he said, giving my mother a kiss.

I asked him why he doesn't just take it back. Mom wouldn't mind. "But I love her," Dad answered, as if that was all the explanation needed.

Now, four years later, the silk Hawaiian shirt still hangs in his closet, pressed between collared dress shirts and formal suit jackets. You'd think my mother would notice he's never worn it. But she doesn't.

*   *   *

Sometimes I look in the mirror and it feels like I am looking at a stranger.

*   *   *

I take Herman for a walk. Herman is my golden retriever and he likes walks, though not long walks in the summertime because it is hot and he is growing old. We walk around the block once. It is not a big block. By the end Herman is trailing behind me, like a quickly-wilting flower, not even bothering to stop and sniff at random bushes. When we get inside the house I clip off his leash and pat him on the head. He has a bald patch and he likes me to scratch him there.

"Good boy, Herman," I say. "Good boy."

*   *   *

He stares straight ahead, face awash in the dim glow from the street-lamp. He taps his thumbs on the steering wheel, a nervous habit. He is beautiful.

"Well," I say, opening the car door. "I'd better go. Thanks for the ride."

"No problem." Suddenly he looks over at me. "Goodbye," he says, and it seems as if he wants to say something more. Like maybe it isn't so simple, maybe life isn't a math equation, maybe two-plus-two doesn't always equal four, maybe…maybe…

It is the nicest thing he's ever said to me.

"Goodbye," I say, climbing out. I shut the door behind me and walk up the driveway, my purse dangling against my right calf. When I reach the doorstep I turn around, just briefly, and glance back. But he's already gone.

How I Became a
Coffee Addict

"Hello?"

A shiver shoots down my spine at the sound of his voice. My heart pounds in my ears, invading my thoughts in the same way a clock's solitary ticking takes over a quiet room when you're (unsuccessfully) trying to fall asleep.

"Hi, Zack," I say. "This is JoAnne."

"Who?"

"Uh, JoAnne."

"I'm sorry, Joanie who?"

"*JoAnne.* Baker."

Silence.

"Remember? From Java Joe's? I'm a, um, 'preferred customer'? I'm tall and blonde and I always order an iced mocha?"

"Oh. Oh…yeah. JoAnne. Of course I remember," he says. But I can tell from his voice that he doesn't.

How can he not remember me? I mean, I've only been going to Java Joe's—the local coffee shop where he works Mondays, Tuesdays and Fridays—to see him nearly every Monday, Tuesday and Friday after school for the past three months and twenty-seven days.

Okay, make that three months and thirteen days—he hasn't been there the last two weeks. At first I thought he was just sick or on vacation, but after awhile I started to get worried. I even went to get coffee on Wednesdays, Thursdays and Saturdays (Joe's is closed on Sundays) in case he changed his working schedule. Still no Zack. I finally mustered up the courage to ask the cashier about him one day as I waited for my iced mocha.

"Zack?" She flashed a wry, knowing smile, looking me over. Her pin-straight hair, streaked with purple highlights, was pulled back into a low ponytail, and she had magenta nail polish and a silver ring on every finger. One of those girls with natural style and ediginess, and an effortless aura of poise. She had a way of making even the bulky green "Java Joe's" apron look unspeakably cool.

I hated her.

"He quit a few weeks ago," Miss Natural Sophistication said, handing me my drink. "He started taking night classes at the college and I guess working just got to be too much."

I realized with embarrassment my mouth was hanging open and I closed it, too quickly, my teeth making a small clicking noise as they snapped together. "Oh. Okay," I stammered, trying to pretend my world hadn't just collapsed. "I, uh, I was just, uh, wondering. I mean, I hadn't seen him here in a while, you know, and I was just, uh, a little curious."

Miss Natural Sophistication raised one of her perfectly-plucked eyebrows a bit but nodded, playing along. I handed her a five-dollar bill and told her to keep the change. I was already out the door and halfway down the block before realizing I forgot to get a straw.

Oh well. I wasn't thirsty anymore, anyway. An iced mocha seems so trivial when you've just lost the love of your life.

Okay, so maybe Zack didn't know that part about being the love of my life. Yet. But things were moving along, we were getting closer, I could feel it. By the time summer rolled around I knew I'd snag a date with him.

That is, until he had to go and ruin it all by enrolling in stupid night classes and quitting his job. Tell me, who needs college, anyhow? Just a waste of time, in my opinion. I mean, Zack was on track to becoming a manager, then maybe owner, and eventually the Donald Trump of the coffee industry! And he threw it all away.

Sorry. Don't mind me. I'm just a little bitter, the same way my grandma likes her coffee—black, without a drop of cream. But you have to understand, Zack was a natural at Java Joe's. He was a gift to society—female society, anyhow—standing there behind the counter and gracing us all with his extremely cool presence. I tell you, Zack is cooler than an iced frapuchino.

Nice, too, and funny. He'd tell you jokes while you waited for your drink. And when he'd write your order down on the slip of paper, he'd also draw you a little cartoon—a dog with big ears or a monkey or even a giraffe. Now, he's no van Gogh, but I still saved every one of those drawings he gave me. I keep them in a shoebox hidden under my bed. Some are duplicates, and on some he spelled my name wrong—Joanie, Janie, even Jody. But I don't care. Because they're from Zack. And Zack was not just perfect at his job—he's perfectly perfect, in every way. I knew it from the moment I first laid eyes on him.

*   *   *

"I hear there's this great new coffee place in the shopping center by the movie theater," my best friend Karina said that lazy December afternoon. We'd spent the past two hours in my room reading old issues of *Seventeen*, giving each other manicures, and planning what to do during Spring Break—even though we both knew we would probably spend Spring Break planning what to do during the summer.

"I don't really like coffee," I said.

"Aww, come on! How can you not like coffee?"

"Easy. I don't like the taste of it."

"Jo, they have these drinks that don't even really taste like coffee at all. They mix in chocolate or vanilla or caramel. Mmmm. Doesn't that sound fabulous?"

"Not really."

"Well, drive *me* there at least, won't you? You can get a scone or something."

I hesitated, glanced over at her. Mistake number one. She looked at me with her puppy-dog-eyed, I-thought-I-was-your-best-friend-in-the-entire-world expression. "*Pleeeeze?* Your mom said you can borrow the car; you might as well take advantage of it. Besides, was it not *me* who babysat David last week so you could go see that lame play you were so obsessed about?"

"*Death of a Salesman* is not lame, Karina! It's Arthur Miller! A classic! It won a Pulitzer Prize, for Pete's sake!"

"Soorrr-ry! Jeez, don't have a cow. What I'm trying to say is, you owe me."

I sighed and looked over at her again. Mistake number two. One more flash of the puppy dog eyes, added to the guilt-trip about babysitting my four-year-old brother "The Terrorizer," whose favorite pastime is putting underwear on his head and pretending to be Spiderman while chasing you around with silly string, and I was history. I dragged myself up off the bed and grabbed the car keys.

"So, Karina, where did you say this place is?"

✳   ✳   ✳

I was expecting a local copycat of Starbucks—you know, cookie-cutter exterior, dim lighting inside with walls painted "eggshell white" and cute little tins of mints on sale by the cash register. Instead, we pulled up to a smallish brick building with vines weaving a web across the outside walls and twinkle lights stretched across a patio area. Inside, more twinkle lights, and a dozen or so small iron tables decorated with colorful mosaic patterns.

The first thing I noticed inside, though, was a giant mural covering the entire far wall. The background was swirls of bold oranges and yellows and reds, painted over with dancing and running silhouette figures, their arms stretched heavenward. The mural is incredibly cheerful, the essence of happiness, and it made me catch my breath and smile. I stood there staring for a moment, transfixed.

The second thing I noticed was Zack—though I didn't know his name was Zack yet. "Pretty incredible, isn't it?" he said, and I turned to see him watching me from behind the counter. Karina was pretending to study the menu posted in block letters above his head, but I could tell she was actually checking out Zack. She looked at me and mouthed the words, "Call a doctor!" It's our secret code for "hot guy alert."

Sometimes Karina can be a little off with her taste in guys, at least in my opinion, but not in this case—at least, in my opinion. Of course, someone would have to be seriously mental not to find Zack seriously good-looking. He had a crisp neatness about him, an All-American boyishness that I loved instantly. Short dark hair, smiling eyes, and dimples.

I am absolutely mad about dimples.

"Uh, yeah. It's amazing," I said, nodding towards the mural. "Who painted it?"

"A friend of mine, if you can believe it," Zack replied. "He's just in college, but he's a really good artist. As you can tell. He even let me help him fill inside some of the lines."

"Wow! I'm impressed!" Karina said with a flirty smile. What was she doing? Didn't she realize Zack was *my* dream guy? Besides, she already had an almost-boyfriend at school. Mark. He plays water polo and has an "outie" belly button that looks just plain weird to me but that Karina thinks is cute. They weren't officially "together," but they had been on a few dates and everyone knew they were practically a couple, even though Mark and Karina wouldn't yet admit it.

"So, what can I get for you ladies today?" Zack asked.

"Let me see…" Karina bit her lip and twirled a strand of long dark hair around her index finger, pretending to be deep in thought. As if this was a major earth-shattering decision, like choosing between "The O.C." and "One Tree Hill", instead of merely weighing the caramel latte against the double mocha.

"I think I'll get…a medium vanilla creme latte with lowfat milk and an extra shot of decaf."

You could tell she wanted to impress him by sounding like a bona-fide coffee expert. I, on the other hand, had absolutely no clue what to get. I stared at the menu, but it was like trying to read a foreign language. I didn't know the difference between a latte and a monkey's butt.

Zack turned to me and inspiration suddenly struck. "Uh, what would *you* suggest?" I asked, hoping I sounded cute and fun and flirty like Karina. He flashed me a smile and it felt like my heart was skipping rope. I gripped the counter with both hands, in case I started to feel faint.

"Jo, I thought you didn't like coffee!" Karina said, tugging my elbow. I shot daggers—sharp ones!—at her with my eyes. "What are you talking about? I love coffee. Coffee, coffee, coffee," I said, turning my attention back to Zack. Karina got the hint. She probably knew if she said anything else I would kick her—and I'm a brown belt in karate.

"Well, if you're like me and love chocolate, a mocha's the thing for you," Zack advised, as though he were sharing a huge secret with me. "I personally like the ice-blended kind, even though it's the middle of winter. I guess I'm kinda weird like that."

"Well, I'm sorta weird myself," I said. "Give me an ice-blended mocha, please."

"For here or to go?" he asked.

"To go," Karina butted in, then looked astonished when I got my eye-daggers back out. "Well, you *do* want to go to the mall, don't you, Jo?" she said, innocent as ever.

When he was ringing up our order at the cash register, Zack asked if either of us wanted to purchase a "preferred customer" card. "It costs just twenty-five bucks a year, and you get twenty percent off every purchase," he explained. *Perfect—it would give me an excuse to go back to Java Joe's!*

"Sounds like a bargain to me!" I said. "I'll take it." I didn't look at Karina—I knew she'd be rolling her eyes. She thinks I let guys have too much control over me. *But this isn't because of Zack,* I told myself. *It's all about the discount on coffee. I mean, really, who can resist such a good deal?* A minor detail that I wasn't sure I even *liked* coffee yet. I would *learn* to like it. After all, I am an experimental person, open to new tastes and possibilities.

Okay, I admit it. It was because of Zack.

"Great! Can I have your phone number?" Zack asked, looking expectantly at me. His eyes were so blue it hurt. My heart starting jumping Double-Dutch. Was this really happening? I must have blushed because Zack said, "It's for the membership card. I need to put your phone number into the computer. You know, for identification purposes."

"Oh!" I felt like such an idiot as I recited the numbers for him. And I had thought that…how could I have thought that?! The worst part was Zack *knew* what I had thought—that he liked me and was going to call and ask me out. How could I be so dumb? Mortified, I swore to myself I would never set foot in Java Joe's again. I'd give Karina the stupid membership card.

Zack rang everything up and we paid. I ended up spending nearly all of my recent babysitting money. Maybe Karina was right. I *do* let guys have too much control over me. Sure, Zack was cute, but there are plenty of other guys out there just as cute. Or even cuter. *That's right*, I told myself. *Even cuter!*

He handed me my ice-blended mocha and our fingers touched. It was like a static electric jolt shooting up my arm. Then he smiled, and suddenly my embarrassment melted away and everything was all right again. I glanced at his nametag and caught "ZACK" spelled out in carefully drawn coffee beans. *Zack.* I rolled the name around in my mind, savoring the sound of it. *Zack. Zack the Coffee Guy.*

"Have a nice day, ladies. Come again soon."

Don't worry, Zack the Coffee Guy, I thought. *We will.*

*   *   *

Or, at least, I would. Once classes started up again in January, Karina had soccer practice every day after school. So I had to go to Java Joe's by myself. I was actually kind of glad. Even though Karina and Mark were now officially dating, Karina is a natural flirt. It was somewhat of a relief to be able to see Zack without having to worry about her stealing his love away from me.

The second time I went to Java Joe's, I spent twenty minutes sitting out in the car trying to get my hair *just right*. And guess what? Zack wasn't there. I was seared with a disappointment so acute I almost turned around and walked right back out of the place without getting anything. But instead, I ordered an ice-blended mocha and further studied the mural as I waited for my drink to be ready.

If you look closely, you can tell the big silhouettes are actually made up of lots of tiny dark figures crammed together. It reminded me of when Karina and I were in second grade and we had coloring book contests, making little dots with the tips of our markers inside the drawn-in lines and seeing how long it took for all the little dots to become one big filled-in shape. Karina always won—I would get frustrated and start to color the normal way after about three minutes of "dotting," as we called it.

I paid for my drink, already feeling like a regular as I used my "preferred customer" card, and waited till I got outside to take a sip. I didn't want to give myself away by making a bitter face. Karina promised me coffee was an acquired taste; it took some getting used to. Well, by golly, I would learn to like it! At least enough to be able to drink it without looking like I had tried a bite of Grandma's spinach surprise. After all, I wanted to be able to start drinking my ice-blended mocha at Java Joe's instead of getting it "to go"—that way I could make my move. Or at least sneak glances at Zack's supreme cuteness for fifteen minutes while I sipped my coffee and tried to work up my nerve.

The second time I saw Zack was the third time I went to Java Joe's. It was a Friday afternoon and I was in kind of a bad mood because I had to babysit The Devil Children that night instead of going out bowling with Karina and some friends.

Why such a terrible nickname? Well, for example, last time I was over the three kids—all under the age of six—managed to drag the garden hose inside the house while I was making macaroni and cheese for dinner. By the time I noticed, the living room looked like a miniature wading pool, and on top of that I burned the macaroni and set off the fire alarm. Needless to say, their mom was not too pleased when she got home. Surprisingly enough, however, she called me the following week to ask if I could babysit again. That tells you how hard it is to find babysitters for The Devil Children. Sometimes I fear their mom will just leave me with them and never come back.

Against my better judgement, I agreed to brave the House of Hades once again. I told myself I was doing a favor for their mom—imagine living with those brats twenty-four/seven! She needed a break. And I needed the money (coffee's not cheap, you know, even with a twenty-percent discount.) One good thing about babysitting bad kids is that the pay is usually pretty good.

Anyway, I went to Java Joe's to get my after-school/pre-migrane coffee jolt. And also to hopefully see Zack. My bad mood evaporated when I opened the door and saw him standing there at the counter. He was chatting with a woman as she paid for her drink. A little kid was with her, probably four years old, maybe five, and he was hiding behind his mother's legs. Every so often he peeked out and looked at Zack, and Zack in turn playfully stuck out his tongue and crossed his eyes at him, and the boy giggled and darted back behind his mother again. I smiled, watching them. Zack had such an effortless charm he could probably make even The Devil Children behave.

I shyly sidled over to the end of the line, pretending to look at the dancing-figures-mural but really watching Zack out of the corner of my eye. He was wearing a green Java Joe's cap that matched his apron, and his dark hair barely peeked out from underneath it. I noticed with a thrill that he had a small silver stud in his left earlobe.

After what seemed like an eternity of waiting—and yet at the same time felt too soon—I was at the front of the line. "What can I get for you, Miss?" Zack asked, and I realized with a sinking heart that he didn't remember me. Well, of course not—why would he? I had been stupid to think he might.

"I'll have, uh, an ice-blended mocha, please," I said, and handed him my "preferred customer" card. He scanned it into the computer and then flashed me a half-smile. "JoAnne Baker," he read from the computer screen as he wrote down my order and passed it to the blender operator. "You came in here a few days ago, right? With your friend?"

"Yeah, that's me!" I said, nearly breathless with surprise and excitement. So he did remember me after all!

"So, I take it you liked the ice-blended mocha?"

"Yeah," I lied, reminding myself to wait to take a sip until I was out the door. "You have good taste."

"What can I say?" He flashed his dimples and handed me my change. My knees wobbled. Moments later, when he gave me my drink, I noticed a cartoon drawing—one of *his* cartoon drawings—on the order slip taped to the side. It was a lizard wearing sunglasses.

Tell me, can you get any cooler than that? A lizard wearing sunglasses! I was so happy that even The Devil Children playing tug-of-war with my sweater and ripping a hole in the armpit didn't ruin my good mood.

After that, I began getting coffee regularly after school. Through a series of trials-and-errors I discovered Zack typically worked Mondays, Tuesdays and Fridays, so I always begged Mom to let me have the car on those days. I was getting to be such a "preferred customer" that Zack soon knew my order by heart.

Before long, I was able to drink my ice-blended mocha without making a face; then I could tolerate it; and finally I actually began to like it. I always chatted with Zack as I ordered and waited beside the counter, and then I would go sit at a table against the far wall and watch him out of the corner of my eye as I finished my drink. I always sipped really, really slowly, pretending to savor every last drop but really savoring my every glimpse of Zack—that is, when I dared to look his way for more than four seconds at a time. It's funny. I thought I was being so extremely obvious with my feelings, but looking back I doubt Zack even thought of me as anything other than your average high school coffee addict.

It's amazing, really, how much you can learn about a person from a ninety-second chat three times a week. I found out that Zack's last name is Blakesford. He graduated the previous year from Huntsville High, the rival school across town—which explains why I'd never seen him around campus. He has an older sister named Janie who lives in Texas with her husband Hank and they are expecting a baby in July. Zack is a die-hard Weezer fan, as well as being an avid Michael Crichton reader, and he loves "Seinfeld."

I had never even heard of Jerry Seinfeld, much less the infamous Kosmo Kramer who Zack found so hilarious, but it wasn't long before I was tuning in at ten o'clock every weeknight so I could laugh along with him the next day while I waited for my ice-blended mocha. I burst with laughter when I got my drink one day and found a cartoon of not a dog or mouse or elephant, but rather a caricature of Kramer sketched on the order slip below my (only slightly misspelled) name.

It was at that moment I knew Zack had become more than just a harmless crush. I could picture Karina rolling her eyes even as I realized the undeniable truth: I was in love. And not just with ice-blended mochas.

*   *   *

Of course, I didn't tell anybody. And Karina was too filled with thoughts of Mark to notice my growing obsession with Java Joe's. For which I was thankful. Her indignant laughter rang in my ears: *"But Jo, you don't even like coffee!"*

If anything, I tried to act more "normal" than ever—which, I should point out, I have never been much good at. But the last thing I wanted was for Zack to discover my true feelings. At least not until he was ready to hear them. Or until I was ready to confess them. Which would not be until, um, forever. Or at least until summer. That would give me about three months to plan out every word I would say, and every possible response he could give, and every word I would use in response to his various possible responses.

There was one afternoon, however, about a week before Zack left Java Joe's, that gave me hope that maybe "summer" would come in March. I had stayed late after school to finish up my science project (The Effects of Coffee on Reflex Time) and it was nearly five o'clock when I pulled into Java Joe's parking lot. I opened the heavy wooden door to find the place deserted. Deserted, that is, except for Zack.

He was washing out a blender in the sink behind the counter. He looked up when the bell hanging above the door announced my arrival. "Hey," he said with a smile that gave me goosebumps all over. "One ice-blended mocha, coming right up."

"You know me too well," I teased. "Maybe one day I'll throw you for a loop and order something different. What do you think of that?"

"I think that would be the end of the world," he teased back. "That would send us into an alternate universe or something."

"Someone has been watching too much Star Trek," I said, sliding along the counter with him as he went over to make my drink.

"Hey, you better watch it," he said, feigning seriousness. "If you're not nice to me, do you know what I'll say?"

"What?"

"No coffee for you!" he yelled in a perfect impression of the "Soup Nazi" from "Seinfeld". I gasped in mock horror. "You wouldn't!"

"I would!" He pressed the blender's ON button with a flourish and shook his finger at me. "You just better stay on my good side, Missy."

I sat down at my usual table, taking indescribably small sips of my ice-blended mocha, while Zack went around wiping down tables. "How come you're here all alone?" I asked, giving myself a mental pat on the back for being brave enough to strike up a conversation instead of merely admiring him from afar like I was prone to doing.

"Oh, Melanie was supposed to be working too," he said, "but she started feeling sick so I told her to go on home and get some rest." He was just two tables away from me now. "I thought I could hold down the fort by myself. Monday's aren't usually too busy for us."

"Yeah," I said, wracking my brain for something else to say, something to keep the conversation going. Out of habit, my gaze shifted to the far wall, finding comfort in the familiar patterns of the mural. I studied it absently for a moment before realizing—*Duh! The mural!*

"So, have you helped your friend paint anything else lately?" I asked, hoping that didn't sound too out-of-the-blue. I told you this acting "normal" thing is a challenge for me.

"Actually, yeah," Zack replied. "I'm helping him with one he's working on right now down at the park close by here—what's that park called? Something with rainbows?"

"Rainbow Bridge?"

"Yeah, that's the one. He's painting—well, what else? A rainbow."

"Oh. That sounds, um, cool."

"Yeah, it is, I guess." Zack was standing right in front of me now, looking down at me with those Caribbean blue eyes. He bent down and started to wipe off my table. He was so close that I could reach out and touch his hair if I wanted to. Actually, I wanted to, but I resisted the urge. I breathed in his spicy cologne mixed with a subtle scent of coffee beans. My heart swooped down to my gut, like I was riding a Six Flags roller coaster with half-a-dozen loop-de-loops.

"I've always liked this mural the best, though," Zack continued, pausing with his dishrag for a moment to look over at the dancing figures. His silver earing glinted in the light from the lamp hanging above us. "It has a message, you know? It touches people, really speaks to them."

"What does it say?"

He turned and looked directly at me. "The people in it, they want you to set your soul free, to be yourself. To open your eyes and open your mind and open your heart and not be afraid. To find joy in life and make the most of every opportunity."

I was filled with such a strong desire to stand up and kiss him that I actually might have done so if only the door hadn't swung open and broken the spell. I swallowed and almost started choking on my drink. In between coughing spasms, I looked up to see the familiar mother and her young son from the other day filling the entryway. Zack glanced over and made a funny face at the little boy as he walked over to take their order behind the counter.

I finished my drink and got up to leave, waving goodbye to Zack as I walked out the door. He smiled at me and I thought, *Wow, he might actually like me.* As impossible as it seemed, it felt like Zack and I had really connected. *We might truly have something special.*

*   *   *

Which is why I was so surprised when I went back to Java Joe's the next day—Tuesday, one of Zack's working days—and found he wasn't there. And why I was even more surprised two agonizing weeks later, when I finally asked about him and discovered he had quit.

What? He can't have quit, I thought. *Why didn't he tell me? We had connected. He could have at least given me a chance to say goodbye.*

I went home and slid the shoebox out from under my bed and looked through my collection of Zack's order slip cartoons. I knew I couldn't let it end, not like this, not without a at least a goodbye.

I looked in the phone book and found three listings for Blakesford. I jotted them down on a scrap of paper and set it out on my dresser and spent the next four days trying to work up the nerve to dial those seven-digit numbers in the hope that one of them was Zack's. I mentally scripted exactly what I would say: "Hi, Zack, this is JoAnne Baker. Yeah, the ice-blended mocha girl. I'm fine, how are you? Well, I just wanted to call because I heard you left Java Joe's and I wanted to wish you good luck with college and everything. What? Oh, yeah, I think I'm free to see a movie on Friday, that sounds great…"

Yeah, I know, that last part was wishful thinking. But after the other day in the coffee shop, I thought our relationship had evolved into something more than just customer and worker; something even more than mere acquaintances, I hoped. Something that was sort of like friends. Right? I mean, we both watched "Seinfeld"! Calling to say goodbye would be the right thing to do in a situation like this. Of course it would. Just the normal thing to do.

You'd think by now I'd quit forgetting that I'm not very good at acting "normal."

From the very beginning, the conversation didn't go as planned.

"JoAnne who?"

I had thought he would at least remember who I was! How could he not remember me? We had shared a deep discussion about a mural only…how long ago was that? Two weeks? Three weeks? Jeez, had it really been three weeks already? Well, you shouldn't forget about someone after only three weeks. Especially if you laughed about "Seinfeld" with that person and drew her cartoons that she saved in a shoebox under her bed.

I saved every last one, you know.

All my carefully-planned words streamed out my mouth in a torrent. I knew I was talking too fast, like I'd guzzled four espressos, but I couldn't help it. I suddenly just wanted to get the conversation over with. "Well-I-was-just-calling-because-I-heard-you-don't-work-at-Java-Joe's-anymore-and-I-just-wanted-to-wish-you-good-luck-with-college-and-everything."

"Oh. Well, thanks. I guess." I could tell he thought I was a psycho stalker. Heck, maybe I am a psycho stalker. I don't even know myself anymore.

"You're welcome."

"Okay."

"Okay."

"Well, goodbye," he said, and I heard a click before I even got a chance to reply.

"Goodbye, Zack," I whispered into the phone, to the person who had slipped so effortlessly out of my life but who won't get out of my head. Or out of my heart.

*   *   *

I tell myself I am never going to make that mistake again. I am never going to let myself fall for some stupid guy I barely know. Do you know what my problem is? It's like Karina says: I let guys have too much control over me. I get a crush on someone and then I build that person up until he seems like the best thing since TiVo and I just start to like him more and more and more. It's a vicious cycle, I tell you. I have to get out. I wonder if it's too late for me to become a nun?

I tell myself that I am going to rip up all of Zack's stupid cartoons, even Kosmo Kramer, and throw them in the trash. Better yet, I'll burn them. Watch them slowly shrivel to a blackened crisp. I get as far as taking the shoebox out from under my bed and lifting the lid. Only the drawing of the lizard wearing sunglasses is smack dab on top of the stack. I sit there looking at it and before I know it I'm crying. Jeez, Zack's so stupid. A lizard wearing sunglasses. What a dork. Only suddenly it seems like the cutest thing in the world.

I gently place the lid on the shoebox and slide it back under my bed.

*   *   *

I tell myself I am never going to set foot in Java Joe's again. What I don't realize, however, is that while I was falling head-over-heels for Zack, I was also falling head-over-heels…

…for coffee. I really have become a full-fledged coffee addict. Laugh it up, Karina.

After a week of driving past Java Joe's on my way home from school, I finally can't take it anymore. Memories flood my mind as I yank open the heavy wooden door and hear the familiar jingling of the bell. I instinctively glance behind the counter, half-expecting to see Zack standing there, even though I wouldn't *want* to see him standing there anymore, not after all that has happened. Or should I say, after all that *hasn't* happened. I still can't believe he didn't even remember me. Am I really that forgettable?

I do a double-take. Wait, is that—no, it can't be. Is it, though? Zack? My heartbeat kicks into a caffeine dance. Maybe there was some sort of mistake, maybe he never really quit at all, maybe I called the wrong number—there could be some other Zack Blakesford living in Huntsville. I mean, it's possible, right? Anything's possible. After all, I've become a bigger coffee addict than Karina, Miss Bona-Fide Coffee Expert Herself.

Then the guy looks up and I see it isn't Zack. What am I talking about, of course it isn't! Zack doesn't work at Java Joe's anymore. He is out of my life. Good riddance, I say.

Yeah, right. Who am I kidding? I feel like crying. I almost turn around and run out of the place right then and there. But the overwhelming aroma of coffee beans sucks me in. I get to the front of the line and hand the guy my "preferred customer" card. He does look a lot like Zack, actually—short dark hair, strong build, Java Joe's cap. Green eyes, though, not blue, and no silver stud earring. Still, he is pretty cute, if you want my opinion.

What am I saying? He's not *that* cute. I refuse to let myself go down this road again. No way. Not ever.

The guy—"JOSH" according to the carefully drawn coffee beans on his nametag—looks a bit lost, so I gently remind him to swipe my card in the special slot by the cash register.

"Sorry about that," he says, embarrassed. "This is my first day, and there's a lot to remember. I pushed the wrong button and charged a lady seventy bucks for a frapachino earlier. Oops." He smiles at me as he hands my card back.

Oh. My. Gosh.

Dimples.

Josh has dimples. I absolutely love dimples.

"So, what can I get for you today?" he asks.

I am about order my usual ice-blended mocha, but for some reason I hesitate. Instinctively, I glance over at the dancing figures silhouetted on the far wall.

The people in it, they want you to set your soul free, to be yourself. To open your eyes and open your mind and open your heart and not be afraid. To find joy in life and make the most of every opportunity.

Yeah, so maybe Zack broke my heart. Maybe I built him up too much in my mind. But should that stop me from giving love another chance? From giving someone else a chance? From maybe even giving myself a chance, too?

I turn and look Josh right in his gorgeous green eyes. Ice-blended mochas are Zack—so yesterday. I want something new.

"Well, Josh," I say with a smile. "What would *you* suggest?"

Red

Grace knocked the nail polish off her bedside table and onto the carpet and that was The End. She crouched there, as if paralyzed, watching the Maybelline "Vixen Red" soak into the white Burbur, the teardrop-shaped stain slowly growing bigger and bigger, like blood seeping into a Band-Aid.

Grace sat there, rocking on her heels, watching and waiting. Waiting and watching. For what, she didn't exactly know. When the teardrop stopped growing, she got up and went to the kitchen to get some paper towels.

✳   ✳   ✳

The rain spattered softly against the car windows. Grace watched the windshield wipers dance, back and forth, forth and back, like her piano teacher's metronome. She sat with her knees hugged up against her chin, trying to minimize the contact of her skin with the cold vinyl. "Mom," she said. "It's raining cats and frogs."

"You mean cats and *dogs*," her mother corrected, never taking her eyes off the road.

It was still raining "cats and frogs" when they arrived at the park. Grace stared out the car window and imagined they were inside a giant aquarium, except filled with birds instead of fish.

Her mother turned around and smiled at Grace in the backseat. "What a perfect day," she said, "to fly a kite!" Grace could tell she wasn't joking. Her mother never joked about important matters.

Part of Grace wanted to stay in the car, but the other part of her won out. She pulled the strings on her sweatshirt hood so tight her face was scrunched and there was only a keyhole of an opening where the rain could get in. Then she tied the strings in a bow— double-knotted, the way Grampa had taught her so it wouldn't come undone.

Grace tightly held her mother's hand as they trudged together up the rain-slickened hill that overlooked the playground. Grace had never been to the park in the rain. It was deserted. Like a magic kingdom that belonged only to Grace and her mother. Just the two of them, and of course some fish disguised as birds. "We've always got each other, Hon," her mom said whenever Grace asked about her daddy. "Us girls gotta stick together. Just you and me, that's all we need."

That's all we need. Just you and me. Grace squeezed her mother's hand.

They were at the top of the hill now, and Grace peeked out her keyhole through the drizzle at the slide and the swingset, then at the picnic tables and the scattered trees, and finally at their blue Volvo parked alongside the curb. Her mother stood a few feet away, face turned skyward, eyes squinting against the driving BBs of water, hair streaming long and wet down her back. Grace's clothes had grown heavy and cumbersome. All the tiny raindrops had banded together. It reminded Grace of one of her Grampa's favorite sayings. "Take little steps, baby steps," he told Grace whenever she was on the brink of giving up. "Baby steps have a way of adding up to a lot of big steps."

"So do raindrops," Grace thought now, wriggling inside her soggy Hello Kitty sweatshirt. "Little raindrops have a way of adding up to big buckets." She wanted to take her sweatshirt off but couldn't get Grampa's double-knotted bow undone. Water ran off the tip of her nose and she stuck out her tongue and caught a drop. She was surprised at how warm it tasted.

Grace's mother held the kite with hopeful outstretched hands. She peered up into the leaden sky as if challenging it, or maybe begging. The kite was small and diamond-shaped and painted with rainbows, which Grace's mother said was "highly ironic." Grace smiled appreciatively even though she didn't know what "ironic" meant. She knew this though: she loved kites and she loved rainbows. And, above all, she loved her mother.

The kite had a hard time getting airborne. "Mom, maybe we should go," Grace said, holding the end of the kite string and shivering slightly, but her mother didn't hear. Grace's mother continued to squint into the drizzle, determined and desperate, holding the kite above her head, quietly beseeching the wind to take the tiny rainbow in its arms and raise it high. Grace knew you shouldn't fly kites in the rain. Her mother knew this too, and yet there she stood, trying anyway. *Just you and me, Hon.* Years later, this was what Grace most vividly remembered when she thought of her mother: eyes squinted toward the heavens, a double-knot bow that just wouldn't come undone, and a tiny rainbow struggling against the rain to fly.

*　　　*　　　*

The chemotherapy started the very next week.

The second time, Grace went with her mother into The Little White Room with the hospital smell and space-age machinery. It reminded Grace of the aliens she had seen once, when her Uncle Bill let her stay up late and watch a movie with The Big Kids. Grace was scared of The Little White Room but she went in anyway. She sat beside the bed and watched the medicine *drip...drip...drip* out of the IV bag, down a clear tube, and into her mother's arm, slowly trickling inside her, becoming a part of her, like blood or bone.

Drip...drip...drip.... It reminded Grace of rain dripping off the leaves of the eucalyptus trees at the park, the day she and her mother flew the rainbow kite. Grace remembered the way her mother shrieked with excitement when the wind finally swept the kite up into its arms. Grace's heart leapt with the thrill of the kite tugging on the string. She forgot about her soggy sweatshirt and stubborn double-knot bow. She and her mother stood side-by-side, *just you and me, Hon,* watching the rainbow dance in the gray misty rain.

"Hey Mom," Grace said now, eyes still transfixed on the IV bag. "It's like the rain."

"That's nice, Honey." But Grace could tell her mother wasn't really listening. She didn't watch the *drip...drip...drip.* Instead, she looked at Grace and asked her questions about kindergarten and play-dates and Grandma and Grampa. She sounded tired.

As the treatments continued, Grace sometimes brought along pictures she drew in art class. This always made her mother smile, except for the picture of the rainbow kite and the rain. That one made her mother cry.

One day when Grace came to The Little White Room she brought a bottle of her mother's nail polish and they painted each other's toenails. Grace was careful as could be, but she still got polish on the skin around her mother's nails. She wasn't very good at "coloring inside the lines," but her mother said that was okay. The nail polish was red; deep red; "Vixen Red." It was her mother's favorite color. She said it made her feel alive. After all, you couldn't be dying if you had bright red toenails. It just didn't fit the picture.

Grace believed her. *We've always got each other, Hon. Just you and me.* She coated her mother's toenails with thick layers of red, as if somehow chip-free nails could create miracles.

And then her mother died, and Grace's eyes were Vixen Red for weeks, and she didn't believe in miracles anymore.

＊   ＊   ＊

Grace kept the $3.49 bottle of Vixen Red polish in her bureau drawer buried underneath her underwear, where nobody would find it. She kept some of her mother's other things—a lock of auburn hair, a lavender silk scarf, a book of Walt Whitman poems—in the drawer of her bedside table. But the nail polish was Grace's secret treasure. Sometimes she would slip it out and painstakingly paint a single fingernail red with the same tiny brush that had traced her mother's nails nearly a decade ago. Now she stayed "inside the lines," carefully painting only one coat, using as little polish as possible, because this was a magical red, her mother's red, and she couldn't go out and buy more when she ran out. She doubted they even made Vixen Red anymore.

Grace would sit there on her bedroom floor, sneaking glances at the splash of vibrant color alive against the white of her skin, stroking the single red nail with her thumb, strangely comforted yet upset with herself at the same time.

Now. Grace watched the pool of Vixen Red soak through the layers of paper towels. The tiny bottle, nearly empty, was propped upright on the bedside table.

She looked out the window. It was raining "cats and frogs." Tears spilled from her eyes and *drip...drip...dripped* down her cheeks, but Grace felt a smile cracking her face. She crawled across the floor and rummaged around in the back of her closet.

Grace sat there for a moment, looking at it, running her hand across the light plastic surface. With Vixen Red-stained fingers, she carefully wiped off a thin film of dust. *Baby steps,* she thought, taking a deep breath. *Baby steps.*

She slipped out the front door and into the rain, hugging the faded rainbow tightly to her chest. *Baby steps. Baby steps.* Grace opened her mouth wide and caught a water droplet on her tongue.

"What a perfect day," she thought, smiling as she squinted into the falling raindrops, "to fly a kite."

WISHING ON
UPSIDE-DOWN
STARS

Derek lived and died with his beloved Cincinnati Reds. Right now he felt like he was on his deathbed.

They were losing. Five runs to a measly two. Bottom of the eighth inning. Game 5 of the World Series. Two runners on base—but also two outs. And knowing Derek's luck, they'd probably get that third out right about…

Derek sat on the couch, perched forward, elbows on his knees, chin in his hands, enraptured in the luminescent glow of the TV screen, watching as the Reds' batter hit a harmless pop fly into the waiting glove of the left-fielder.

…*now*.

Derek groaned and clicked the mute button, silencing the commentary of the television broadcasters who, at least to Derek's ears, knew as much about baseball as he knew about knitting. Which was next to nothing. His grandma tried to teach him one time—she had always wished for a granddaughter and was so excited when Derek's mom got pregnant a few years ago and the ultrasound showed it was a girl. Two weeks later Derek's mom had a miscarriage. And so Derek was all his grandma got, was all his parents got, was all he himself got. He tried his best to fill the void, but some things—knitting, for example—are just best left to girls.

"What's the score?" Derek's dad asked, cracking open an after-dinner beer—"Budweiser, Official Beer of the World Series"—and plopping down beside him on the couch.

"Still five to two, New York," Derek replied, wishing *he* were old enough to drink and drown his sorrows. He glanced over at his father. Dad was wearing a battered Cincinnati Reds cap—

"my lucky Johnny Bench hat," he called it. Only it wasn't very lucky, at least as far as Derek could tell. Cincinnati hadn't made it to the World Series since before Derek was born. And now, when they finally *did* make it, it appeared it was once again time to "wait till next year." Sure, Cincy had gotten off to a promising start when they won the first game of the Series thanks to a shutout by star left-hander Clyde Hudson. But then the Reds' pitching arms suddenly lost their aim and a thief seemingly stole the Reds' sluggers' bats out of the dugout. It was like they were just waiting for New York to come back and stomp all over them. Which, of course, those Damn Yankees were doing.

Humiliating. *Wait till next year.* More like next *decade.*

"Hey, where's the sound?" Derek's dad asked, grabbing the controller and clicking off the mute.

"Cincinnati has its back to the wall tonight," said the broadcaster. The cliché felt like a punch in Derek's stomach. He resisted the urge to throw his shoe at the television screen. Why was he even watching anymore? This was hopeless.

"This is hopeless, Dad," Derek said, sighing and getting up from the couch. "It's too painful to watch. I'll be in my room."

"Suit yourself, Son."

A wave of cheers echoed down the hallway and filled Derek's ears, the broadcasters' polished voices barely audible above the roar of screaming Yankee fans. Derek stomped upstairs, thinking how much he despised the Yankees. He hated their fans even more. Always gloating from up there on their high-and-mighty horse, thinking they're better than everyone else just because their owner George Steinbreiner buys the title every year. So what? Anyone can see Cincy would be head and shoulders above those Yankees if only home-run slugger "Big Frank" Fletcher hadn't injured his shoulder mid-season and been out for the rest of the year.

"Baseball's a lot like life, Derek," his dad said when they had heard the news that the Reds' star first baseman was officially Done For The Season. "Sometimes it just ain't fair."

The words weren't very consoling at the time, and they certainly weren't any more comforting now. If only Derek's life was a movie. Then the Reds would make a miraculous comeback and end up winning the game. Maybe Big Frank's replacement would hit a dramatic bottom-of-the-ninth, two-out Grand Slam. Yeah, that would be sweet. And then they'd ride the momentum and rally to win the Series. They'd finally be Champs. World Champs. The Big Red Machine once more. And Derek, number-one-devoted-fan-since-the-day-he-was-born-and-his-parents-dressed-him-in-a-little-Cincinnati-Reds-baby-outfit, would feel like a Champ himself.

And the crowd goes wild!!! That's how movies always end, baseball movies, underdog-winning-despite-the-odds movies. Happy endings. "The End" in gold letters. A perfect package with all the strings tied up. No loose ends. The bad guys punished, the good guys heroes. The Yankees lose, the Reds victorious. The End.

But life isn't a movie. Derek already knew that. If his life were a movie, he'd have a kid sister now, and his grandma would have someone to teach how to knit, and his mother wouldn't get all quiet and leave the room every time she saw a commercial for diapers or baby shampoo. Dad was right—life sure isn't fair.

Derek did a bellyflop onto his bed, like a healthy Big Frank sliding head-first into second base, then rolled over, wiggling his toes in his socks and tilting his head back so he could see the stars out his bedroom window. He liked watching the world upside-down; things looked so much nicer that way. Less serious. It's hard, for example, to stay in a bad mood when you're watching people run upside-down on a grass ceiling. That's what he saw after baseball practice every school day, when he stretched his legs and put his head on the ground and looked upside-down at the track team jogging around the field.

Actually, Derek usually watched one person. Regina Phillips. Most people looked goofy running upside-down, but she looked cute. Prancing across the grass, lightly, effortlessly, like a deer with feathers for feet.

The stars seemed especially bright tonight. Derek's grandma always wished on stars, though a lot of good that did during his mom's pregnancy. Still, she swore there was "some sort of magic at work up there." Derek, still on his back, gazed out his window and wondered if upside-down stars were even luckier than normal stars. Might as well give it a shot. He closed his eyes. *I wish…* he thought. *I wish Regina…*

"Derek! Derek, come down here! You've gotta see this!"

Derek's eyes jerked open. He bolted off his bed and rushed downstairs two-steps-at-a-time into the family room, sliding across the smooth wood floor in his socks. A lump of hope rose in his throat. Maybe his grandma was right. Maybe there was some sort of magic at work up there.

"Reds 've got two runners with two outs," Derek's dad said, eyes glinting with excitement. "The Yanks' pitcher suddenly can't find the strike zone. It's still a long shot, but there's hope. There's always hope, Son."

Derek sat down beside his dad, perched forward, elbows on his knees, chin in his hands, enraptured once again in the luminescent glow of the TV screen. Maybe…

The batter hit a laser-beam to right field. A run for Cincinnati! Now the score was five to three. Still two men on. Still one out left. *There's always hope, Son.* Maybe…

"C'mon, c'mon," Derek whispered to himself, to the television screen, as if his team could hear, as if he could send telepathic messages all the way to New York. "Just a couple more runs."

The batter swung and missed; strike one. "C'mon, c'mon…"

On the next pitch the batter made contact, but the ball soared off to the left side and into the crowd. Foul ball; strike two.

"The Yankees are one strike away from a World Championship…" said the broadcaster.

Derek wiggled his toes in his socks, nervous energy squirming inside his stomach like worms. He felt sick.

Please, please…let him get a hit, he prayed, to God, to himself, to anyone who was listening. His mother would be upset if she knew—"You don't waste prayers on silly baseball games!"—but she didn't understand. To Derek this wasn't just a *silly* baseball game; it was his team, his dream, the World Series! Opportunities like this don't come along every day.

Another pitch; Derek held his breath. Ball one. He closed his eyes and sighed with momentary relief.

If Cincinnati wins, I'll do anything, Derek pleaded in his mind, desperately searching for something to risk, something to bet, something that would convince the Baseball Gods to answer his prayer. His mind settled on the one thing—besides baseball, of course— that was always at the forefront of his mind: Regina. *If Cincinnati wins, I'll talk to Regina.*

The sharp crack of a bat over the roar of the crowd jolted Derek out of his daydream. He opened his eyes to see the baseball soaring towards the outfield fence. *Going…going…*

"GONE!" screamed the television broadcaster as the crowd erupted in a riot of noise. "I DON'T BELIEVE IT! CINCINNATI HAS COME BACK TO WIN THE GAME! THIS SERIES IS STILL ALIVE, FOLKS!"

"Hoo-boy, Derek! *Hoo-boy!*" his dad exclaimed, jumping up off the couch and spilling his beer in excitement.

"Yeah, Dad! Hoo-boy! I can't believe it! We won! WE! HOO! BOY! WON!" Derek danced around the room, high-fived and hugged his dad, slid into the kitchen and high-fived and kissed his mom. "We won, Mom! Hoo-boy! We're still alive!"

It wasn't until later that night, when Derek was lying in bed, his head tilted back to stare at the upside-down stars before he drifted off to sleep, that he remembered. *If Cincinnati wins, I'll talk to Regina.* The squirming worms suddenly invaded his stomach again.

Cincy may still be alive, Derek thought, *but tomorrow I am going to die of nerves.*

*   *   *

The problem was this: Derek had never talked to Regina. Not once. Not ever. Not even a hello.

He knew her, of course. From afar. He knew she liked to wear her long chestnut hair parted on the left side and pulled back into a low ponytail. On foggy days little curls would spring up in the strands around her face, which she was always trying to smooth down with her hands. Maybe if—no, Derek told himself, *when*—he talked to her, he would tell her to stop doing that. He liked her curls.

Derek knew Regina had a locker six to the right of his and that she always arrived at school just as he was shutting his own locker to head off to class. He tried getting to school a few minutes later, tried opening his locker incredibly slowly, even tried shutting his locker and then pretending he had forgotten something and opening it again, but his timing was never quite right. Regina was an unbelievably slow locker-opener. Sometimes, Derek saw as he watched her out of the corner of his eye, she had to rotate the lock numbers to her combination three times before finally getting that stubborn lock to click open. Once he almost went over and asked if she needed help, but then a friend of hers walked up and the moment was lost. It seemed Derek was always losing moments; he imagined them as coins slipping out of a hole in his pocket, leaving a shining trail of missed opportunities behind him.

Derek knew Regina had a lot of friends. That, in fact, was part of the problem. Because it seemed someone was always with her. *What is it with girls*, he thought, *that makes them so terrified to be alone? They even walk to the bathroom in groups!* Anyway, it was scary enough to think of going up to her when she was alone; if her friends were there too, such bravery was out of the question. *C'mon,* he silently told the Baseball Gods, *you've gotta be reasonable. That would be like asking me to root for the Yankees. Some things just CAN'T be done.*

So, Derek figured as he sat in English class pretending to take notes about the difference between simile and metaphor, if—no, *when!*—he was going to talk to Regina, this would be the perfect time to do it. He stole a glance at her, which wasn't too hard considering she sat directly across the aisle from him. She was wearing a blue sweater today and there were curls in her hair. The worms were back, squirming around in his stomach. God, she killed him.

Suddenly Regina glanced up, caught him looking, and…

…smiled at him. *Smile back, smile back!* Derek told himself, but the synapses and neurons didn't deliver the urgent message to his face. Instead, he panicked and shifted his gaze to the clock on the wall behind her, pretending to be extremely interested in the time. 1:43. Only seventeen minutes of class left. And then Derek would make his move.

Hoo-boy, as his dad would say. *There's always hope.*

Focus, focus, Derek told himself. *What are you going to say to her? You must have a plan, a script. Otherwise you'll say something stupid. Or worse, chicken out. Yes, you will. You know you will. But you're not going to. You're going to talk to her. Hoo-boy, you're going to talk to Regina Phillips…*

"Derek, could you please give us an example of a simile?"

Derek's head jerked up like he'd been zapped with two-hundred-and-twenty volts of electricity. Mrs. Singer was looking at him with that tight-lipped smile that said, *I know you haven't been listening and now it's your time to pay.* God, Derek hated that smirk. He swore teachers had a sixth-sense: they could detect daydreaming the way sharks could smell blood in the water.

"A…a…simile?" Derek repeated, skimming over his notes. "Okay, um…" *Think, think!* Across the aisle Regina smiled at him encouragingly.

"Her smile…is like a grand slam in the bottom of the ninth inning," Derek blurted out, "…when the crowd is going crazy but all you can hear is the beating of your heart…and you realize that this is what it truly means to be alive."

Derek felt all the class looking at him. His cheeks grew hot and he couldn't meet Regina's eyes. Oh God, why had he said that? Now she knew. Now everyone knew. He felt exposed, naked. He wished he could shrink and fall through a crack in the floor into nothingness.

"That was excellent, Derek. Thank you," said Mrs. Singer. "Okay, now…Erin, could you give us an example of a metaphor?"

Derek hadn't realized his shoulders were tensed up until felt them relax. Mrs. Singer had found a new victim; she would probably leave Derek alone for the rest of the period. He glanced at the clock. 1:48. Twelve more minutes. Twelve measly minutes to come up with something to say to Regina Phillips, the girl he had spent this entire freshman year admiring. From afar.

It reminded him of baseball tryouts. You spend your whole Little League and youth careers building up to high school, and the entire time you're thinking, *later, later, I'll practice that later, I'll figure that out later, late*r. And even though you're working towards a goal, it's a distant goal, barely within your sight. But then suddenly *later* is *now* and you find yourself sitting in the dugout waiting for your turn at bat and your palms are sweaty and the bat feels like heavier than a sledgehammer and you wonder how you will find the strength to *swing*, much less get a hit. You look around at the other guys, and though rationality tells you they're as nervous as you are, they don't seem nervous in the least; they seem mature and confident and prepared. You don't feel good enough. At all.

That was like trying to talk to Regina. Nothing he could think to say seemed good enough. At all.

Across the aisle, she was absentmindedly fiddling with a loose piece of yarn that had unraveled from her sweater, wrapping it around her finger the same way Derek was wrapped around her finger. And she didn't even know it.

Hoo-boy. She killed him.

*　　　*　　　*

R-I-I-I-ING!!! Students got up from their desks, slung backpacks that seemed to weigh eighty pounds over their shoulders, and lumbered out the door to afternoon's short-lived freedom. Derek wanted to sprint after them, but instead he took three steps across the aisle to where Regina was zipping up her backpack.

Derek stood there a moment, summoning his courage like he did when he stepped into the batter's box against a hard-throwing pitcher. He wanted to turn and run for the door with the speed he usually reserved for trying to steal a base. But the Baseball Gods were merciless. So. Derek took a deep breath. Then:

Regina looked up. "Hi, Derek," she said.

"Hey," Derek replied, his voice so hoarse it sounded like he hadn't talked in days. He tried to smile but his face felt stiff—*like a baseball mitt before it's been broken in*, was the simile that flashed through his mind.

"What class do you have next?" Regina asked, standing up, her green eyes meeting his. *Hoo-boy.*

"Baseball practice," Derek managed to reply.

"I didn't know you played ball!" she said. "Cool. Well, I have track practice and that's up at the field too. I'll walk with you?"

She said it like a question. Did that mean he was supposed to answer? Derek nodded his head, but Regina didn't see because she was already beginning to walk towards the door. Derek caught up to her, feeling almost dizzy, as if he was in a dream, or in a movie, watching an actor play himself on the big screen.

And the crowd goes wild…

But his life wasn't a movie. Derek should know that by now.

"I really liked your simile," Regina said.

Derek felt his face grow hot again, about a hundred degrees hotter than twelve minutes ago. She knew. She had to know.

"Oh, yeah, um, thanks," he mumbled, looking at his Nikes.

A pause. The pair walked along in silence for a few moments. To Derek, it felt as long as Christmas Eve feels to a five-year-old. He desperately searched his mental hard-drive for something to say, but his computer was frozen, everything had vaporized into mist, melted into puddles, flown away like caged birds being set free. His mind was filled with similes, but no small talk. Then:

"So, I take it you watched the game last night?" Regina asked, smiling at him as they walked side-by-side down the hallway, through the crowds of students yelling and laughing and rumbling on home—though to Derek it felt like it was only him and Regina, alone in the world.

"The World Series, you mean? Yeah, of course I did! Wasn't it...

"...awesome?" Derek said.

"...awful?" Regina said.

They looked at each other.

"Wait, you *like* Cincinnati?" she asked incredulously.

"You like the *Yankees*?"

"Of course!" Regina replied with passion. "I used to live in New York. Heck, my dad is such a Yankees fan he named me after Reggie Jackson! He wanted a boy, got me instead, so Regina it was. He calls me Reg-GIE anyway."

"Well, I've been a Reds fan since the day I was born," countered Derek, the worms that seconds before had been squirming around inside his stomach now suddenly gone. He could argue about baseball with the President of the United States and not be nervous. The Reds were his team. His dream.

"I'm sorry to break this to ya, Derek, but your team's gonna get it tonight," Regina playfully trash-talked. "My Yanks were feeling sorry for your Reds; wanted to drag the Series out a little longer. But tonight they'll finish 'em off."

"I wouldn't be so sure about that, Reg-GIE!" Derek teased back. "You're just like those Yankees you love so much—too cocky. My team's gonna knock you down off that high horse you're riding on. You'll see."

"Is that what you think? Oh, Derek, you're in *total* denial. You're living in a fantasy world."

"Okay," Derek found himself saying. "I'll bet you. If your Yankees win, I'll buy you lunch."

"And if the Reds hang on for one more game, lunch is on me. It's a deal."

"Deal."

"Okay then. See ya tomorrow," Regina said, heading towards the girls' locker room while Derek went across the field to the boys'. Suddenly:

"Derek!" Regina called. He turned. "I'm looking forward to that lunch you're gonna buy me tomorrow!" She smiled, waved, then turned and jogged towards the locker room.

Hoo-boy. She killed him.

*   *   *

Derek's grandmother always said that "to make God laugh, you just gotta tell Him your plans."

Derek never really understood that. Until now.

The love of his life, a Yankees fan?!

The Baseball Gods must be laughing pretty hard, he thought.

*   *   *

That night, as he sat on the couch beside his dad, watching Cincinnati get tromped in Game 6 by the Yanks, four-to-one, Derek thought about the way Regina would gloat tomorrow at school when he bought her lunch. He smiled to himself, shaking his head, remembering her teasing laugh, her incredulous expression, "You *like* Cincinnati?" She was going to rub salt in his wound, Derek knew. Probably order everything on the cafeteria menu. Those Yankee fans are the worst.

Derek's cheeks felt like they had been microwaved for fifteen seconds as he imagined Regina sitting across from him in the cafeteria and then, if there was indeed some magic at work in those upside-down stars, walking with him to English class fifth period. Curls in her hair, twirling a loose string on her sweater. Hoo-boy. A Yankees fan. Who would have guessed?

Derek punched the mute button on the TV. Sound was too painful. He hated watching the Reds lose.

"I hate seeing the Reds lose, Dad," he said. His father just sighed sympathetically.

"Well, we gave 'em a run for their money at least, didn't we, Son?"

A run for their money. Derek hated that expression. It was simply a nice way of saying, "We lost." It certainly looked like Cincy was a goner. Which, quite frankly, sucked. Especially when they had come so close, made it to the World Series, were only two games away from being Champs-with-a-capital-C.

It was even more painful for Derek to watch now, knowing that when the World Series was over so would his relationship—if you could even call their mild bantering a relationship—with Regina be over, too. After all, what would he talk to her about besides baseball? How would he ever sit with her at lunch if it wasn't because of a bet?

If the Reds win tonight and force a final Game 7, Derek silently pleaded, though he knew it was hopeless, the last time was just a fluke, pure luck that had nothing to do with his desperate wishing...but still...*If the Reds win tonight, I'll...*think, think!...*I'll talk to Regina again. I'll walk with her to practice. I'll...I'll ask her to do something. With me. Like hang out or something. That's it! If the Reds rally and win tonight, I'll ask Regina to hang out with me.*

The Baseball Gods listened to his plea before, didn't they? And he did his part by talking to Regina. But Derek knew if his life were a movie he wouldn't need to offer up another promise to the Baseball Gods and another Reds' victory to ask Regina out. If his life were a movie he would have the guts to take his little triumph today and run with it, run with it like he was trying to stretch a double into a triple. If his life were a movie he would keep talking to Regina even after the Series ended, and he'd become friends with her instead of just stealing glances at her across the aisle in class or watching her run upside-down across the field after practice.

But life isn't a movie. And Derek knew that this was hopeless, his Reds would lose, he would go back to being a shy admirer from afar. And that would be The End.

This was The End.

The End.

Goodbye, Regina. Good...

*   *   *

"...BYE, MR. BASEBALL!!! I DON'T BELIEVE IT FOLKS, A GRAND SLAM!!! THE REDS HAVE DONE IT AGAIN! THERE MUST BE MAGIC IN THEIR GATORADE, BOB!"

"SURE SEEMS SO, RALPH...THIS IS A WHOLE NEW SERIES, FOLKS! IT'S GONNA COME DOWN TO THE DECISIVE GAME SEVEN FRIDAY NIGHT IN CINCINNATI, WHICH, OF COURSE, WILL BE TELEVISED RIGHT HERE ON YOUR FAVORITE SPORTS CHANNEL..."

*   *   *

There was a spot of ketchup above Regina's upper lip, to the right. Derek wanted to reach over and gently wipe it off, but he didn't of course. He didn't even tell Regina it was there. Why embarrass her? Besides, he thought it was cute. Just like the curls in her hair.

It drove him crazy, that little blop of red below her nose, like a freckle, or like one of those "beauty marks" his mom was always drawing on her cheek with an eyebrow pencil. He asked her about it once. Her being his mom. She got a little embarrassed and said it made her more attractive, didn't he see, but he wouldn't understand, it's just something women do, now go outside and play. She was right, Derek didn't understand. Now, though, seeing that tiny pinprick of ketchup above Regina's upper lip, he thought maybe he did.

Hoo-boy.

"You are sooooo lucky, Derek," Regina said, wiping her mouth with a napkin and suddenly erasing the beauty mark she didn't even know she had. *That's okay,* Derek thought. *She's still beautiful.* "I thought my Yanks had it clinched for sure. We should have taken our pitcher out sooner, you could tell he was gettin' tired. But who would have thought, a grand slam? Your Reds are just so stinkin' lucky!"

Derek smiled, dipped a couple of French fries in a thousand pinpricks of ketchup. "What can I say? Pure skills, Reg-GIE, pure skills."

"Just listen to you, Mr. Hot-Shot!" she exclaimed, flinging her bunched-up napkin at him like a playful brushback pitch. "Last night was a fluke. An unfortunate accident."

"Serendipity."

"No, that's a *fortunate* accident."

"It was fortunate for me," Derek said with a grin.

"Yeah, well, I think something's screwy. Like, have you ever seen that movie *Angels in the Outfield?* That's what this reminds me of. Unbelievable luck. It's like the Baseball Gods are smiling on your Reds for some reason."

"Yeah," Derek said, draining the last of his milk. "Only real life isn't a movie."

"I don't know," Regina said, looking across the table at him in a funny way that made Derek suddenly wonder if *he* had ketchup on his face. "Sometimes life will surprise you."

*   *   *

Derek put off asking Regina during lunch. He put off asking her while they walked to class together. He put off asking her for as long as he dared.

Before Derek knew it they were in fifth period, sitting in their desks across the aisle from each other, and Mrs. Singer was picking parts for *Othello*. Derek sighed to himself, wondering if he had lost his chance, left another path of shining coins like footprints trailing behind him. During lunch he had half-a-dozen perfect opportunities to ask Regina to do something, to appease the Baseball Gods so that maybe—just maybe—Cincy would win tomorrow, and they would be Champs, and he would be Champ, too, and then maybe—just maybe—he would be brave enough to tell Regina how he felt about her. Straightforward, this time. Not in a stupid simile.

Now that would never happen. Because he had blown it. *I'm sorry*, Derek pleaded in his mind to the Baseball Gods, *I'm sorry! Just give me one more chance. I promise I'll come through, if I just have one more chance...*

"Derek, we haven't heard from you in a while. Why don't you read the part of Othello for us?" said Mrs. Singer, smiling her tight-lipped smile at him. Derek nodded, swallowed, leafed through the pages of his book to Act V. The worms were back in his stomach, break-dancing, making him want to throw up. He always got so nervous, reading in class. Always afraid he would make a fool of himself, stumble over words, mispronounce things—strike out, so to speak.

"And let's see, who will read the part of Desdemona?" Mrs. Singer continued, looking around the room for another victim. "Ah! Regina. You haven't read yet, have you? Okay, that's perfect. Regina will read the part of Desdemona."

Derek met Regina's green eyes briefly across the aisle. His words echoed in his mind. *I promise I'll do it, if I just have one more chance…*

He knew this was his chance. *If you want to make God laugh, you just gotta tell Him your plans.* Derek sighed to himself. Just his luck that the Baseball Gods thought they were funnier than Adam Sandler.

$$* \qquad * \qquad *$$

"Sorry I killed you."

Derek said this quickly, almost like one word—"SorryIkilledyou"—before he could think to turn away from Regina's desk and sprint out the classroom door to freedom.

"In the play, I mean. Sorry I killed you in the play," he continued, feeling unbelievably vulnerable. He always felt vulnerable, around Regina. It made him uneasy, afraid almost, though at the same time he felt wide-awake, like he had chugged four Red Bulls. Like ameobas, the worms in his stomach had split in half and multiplied.

Regina laughed as she hoisted her backpack onto her shoulder. "It's okay," she said, feigning seriousness. "It was just a misunderstanding." She took a few steps toward the door. Derek stood frozen, rooted to the spot. *Just give me one more chance.* This was that chance. His last chance. He took a deep breath and got ready to swing for the fences. Then:

"Hey, Regina! You coming?"

Derek and Regina both turned to see Josh Reinheart waiting outside the open classroom door. Josh was a senior; Student Body Vice President; star pitcher on the Varsity baseball team; a true Big Man On Campus. Derek hadn't spoken two words to the guy, but he did walk by him in the halls sometimes—or rather, passed by Josh's always-present entourage of fellow star athletes and giggling girls. Today, Josh was wearing a baseball cap—a *Yankees* cap—and sunglasses even though the sky was overcast. He also wore a slightly arrogant smile, as if he was secretly laughing at everyone behind their backs. Derek felt as if that smile was aimed right at him.

"Just a sec, Josh!" Regina called, giving Derek a quick wave good-bye before practically skipping out the door. She looked so excited to see Mr. Popular it made Derek's stomach clench, the same way it had two years ago when his still-pregnant mom had come home from her routine doctor's appointment, her eyes red and swollen from crying. Derek felt like such an idiot for thinking he had a chance with Regina just because they had made a couple silly bets on the World Series. Why would she even give him a second thought if she had guys like Josh Reinheart after her?

Derek sighed. Things like this never happened in movies. If his life were a movie, Derek would be the hero. He would get the girl.

But Derek's chance to ask Regina out had been snatched away. Not that he thought she'd say yes—he wasn't kidding himself anymore—he just wanted to fulfill his promise to the Baseball Gods. Then maybe, just maybe, Cincy would win tomorrow night. And then, even without Regina, Derek would maybe—finally—feel like a Champ.

*   *   *

"Hey, Derek!" Regina called, jogging to catch up to him after class the next day. Derek forced a smile. He didn't want her to know anything was different; didn't want her to think he had thought he stood a chance with her; didn't want her to guess he had interpreted their new friendship as being anything more than just that. A friendship.

"So, are you ready to watch your Reds lose tonight?" Regina said, a teasing smile making her dimples double in cuteness.

Instantly, Derek knew exactly what he had to do. Sure, she was going to turn him down and it would be embarrassing and awkward, but then at least he would be keeping his promise to the Baseball Gods. And maybe, just maybe, Cincy would win tonight.

Regina smiled at him, waiting for his retort.

So. Derek played his role. "I'm sorry to break this to ya, Regina," he playfully scoffed, "but I think *you're* the one in Fantasyland. Cincy's on a roll. We're gonna win Game 7 and take the title tonight."

"Is that what you think, Mister Hot-Shot? Win a few games and suddenly you're all cocky? Well, you just wait and see. My Yanks are gonna knock you down off *your* high horse."

"Oh Reg-GIE, you're in *total* denial."

"Okay, Der-REK," she said, her eyes meeting his. "I'll bet you."

"You're on."

"When my Yankees win—"

"You mean *if* your Yankees win. A very slight *if*."

She rolled her eyes. "*When* my Yankees win," she repeated, with emphasis. "You take me out to lunch."

Derek swallowed. "Only this time," he said, "…it'll be a date."

Regina stopped in her tracks, searching his face. She smiled hesitantly. Was that pity he saw in her eyes? "Okay," she said softly. Then:

"Regina, what are you doing tonight? I mean, where are you watching the game?"

Derek couldn't believe the words were actually coming from his mouth. He told himself it was because of the Baseball Gods. Had it counted before, when Regina brought up the bet and he just called it a "date"? Derek wasn't sure. He figured he might as well seal the deal, so there would be no question about it. He would follow through on his part of the pact.

"Because I was wondering," Derek continued, barely pausing for breath, "if you wanted to come over. And, you know. Watch the game. With, um. Me?"

He looked at his Nikes, bracing himself for the rejection he knew was coming. She didn't say anything. For what seemed like minutes, hours, days. Then:

"Sure," Regina said.

"Oh," Derek said, trying not to sound surprised. "Okay. Well, um—okay. See you at my house at eight?"

"Eight. I'll be there." Then Regina turned and headed towards the girls' locker room. Derek watched her for a moment before turning and walking the opposite direction on two solid—okay, slightly-wobbly—legs across the grassy sports field.

It wasn't until a few minutes later, when he was in the locker room lacing up his baseball cleats, that Derek fully realized what he had done. It was bittersweet knowing Regina didn't feel the same way about him that he felt about her, that those worms didn't crawl inside her stomach when she was around him, that she didn't tilt her head back and wish on upside-down stars that she could spend a moment in his company. And yet, despite all that…

…*Hoo boy!* Derek couldn't wait to watch the game with her.

*   *   *

Derek's mother was straightening up the house. It's what she always did when she was nervous, or sad. Place the magazines on the coffee table in an even stack, fold the two afghans Grandma had knitted and lay them neatly across the back of the couch, rearrange the picture frames on the mantel. Finally, she looked up at him.

"Well, Derek, I think that's nice you're having this girl over. I'm looking forward to meeting her."

"Mom," Derek sighed. "You can stop trying to act all fine with this. I know you're sad. I just don't understand why."

"I'm not sad."

"Yes you are."

"Why would you think that?"

"Because, I can just tell. You're straightening up."

His mother put down the pillow she was fluffing. "And what is wrong with my straightening up a bit?"

"You always do it when you're sad about something." Derek swallowed, meaning to stop, to leave it at that, but then he felt the words gushing out of him, like the dam inside him had burst when he asked Regina out. "You cleaned nonstop for weeks after the baby…after you lost the baby."

His mother just stared at him. "Derek…"

"And mom, I'm sorry about the baby. I'm so, so, SO sorry. I'm sorry I can't knit for Grandma. I'm sorry Dad won't be able to walk me down the aisle someday. I'm sorry I can't go shopping with you, or get our nails done, or whatever it is that mothers and daughters do together. I'm sorry, Mom. I'm sorry everyone's stuck with me. With just me."

He swallowed. His mother looked like she had been punched in the stomach. Derek felt the tears burning behind his eyelids but he willed them to stay back.

"I'm sorry, Mom…"

"No," she said, crossing over to him. "I'm the one who's sorry."

"Listen, Derek…we were sad when we lost the baby, very sad, because we had been so excited to add a new member to our family. But in no way does that mean that we're not happy with the way our family is, or that we're not happy with you. Your father and I love you so much, Derek," she said, hugging him now, and Derek felt the tears sliding down his face. "And just the way that a baby wouldn't change that…*no* baby doesn't change that, either. Nothing could ever change that."

She pulled away from him, and her face was wet, too, and her eyes were swollen and red, but she was smiling. "I'm just straightening up a bit," she explained, refolding the afghans on the couch. "Because I don't want this *friend* you're having over to think we're slobs." She paused a moment, then looked at her son, a mischievous glint in her eye. "Because, Derek," she said, "we all know this is more than just a baseball buddy coming over to watch the game."

"Mom, it's really no big deal," he said, not meaning a word. And his mom knew it.

"Now, Derek, I'll have none of that. I'm your mother. Tell me about this girl."

Derek felt his cheeks grow hot, the same way they always did when he thought of *this girl*. The girl. His girl, at least for this one evening. He smiled. "Hoo-boy, Mom. Just wait'll you meet her."

*   *   *

Regina was wearing her blue sweater. And a Yankees baseball cap.

"I'm sorry," Derek said, pointing at the hat. "You can't wear that in this house."

"Is that the way you greet a guest who comes to your front door?"

"You can just leave it outside and get it when you leave."

"But this is my lucky hat!"

Derek grinned. "Then I really think you should get rid of it. Just my advice. I mean, it hasn't been very lucky the last two games, eh?"

She stuck her tongue out at him before following him inside, "NY" cap pressed firmly to her head.

*   *   *

The Reds were losing.

Four runs to a measly one. Bottom of the ninth inning.

"Who's lucky now, eh, Derek?" Regina said, smirking at him. Derek sighed. Even her smirk made his legs turn to Silly Putty. He was glad they were sitting down.

"Don't be so sure, Regina," he said. "We've still got a chance. Two runners on base. There's always hope."

"Oh, Derek, you're in *total* denial. You're in Fantasyland."

"Whatever you say, Miss Reg-GIE Jackson."

A pause. They sat there, side-by-side on the couch, both perched forward, elbows on knees, chin in hands, enraptured in the luminescent glow of the TV screen. The Reds' batter hit a line drive.

"Bases loaded, Regina! Gettin' nervous?"

"Two outs, Derek. You're the one who should be shakin'." She fingered the bill of her lucky Yankees cap, refusing to look at him. Then:

"But Derek, I was just thinking...we never decided what you would get. If you win the bet, I mean."

"*When* I win the bet."

"*If* you win the bet. And it's a very slight *if*."

Derek smiled to himself. *I feel like I've already won*, he thought.

"I feel like I've already won," he found himself saying, the words rolling off his tongue before he could reel them back in.

"Aww, Derek," Regina said, looking at him and—were his eyes playing tricks?—scooting a little bit closer on the couch. "That's so sweet. Like a line from a movie. I almost forgive you for being a Reds fan. Almost."

"Very funny," Derek said, heart pounding double-time. He tried to focus back on the game. *C'mon*, he told himself, *c'mon, this is the World Series! Opportunities like this don't come around every day. Cincy has a chance to be Champs! World Champs! And you have a chance to be Champ, too.*

"Well, I guess we'll just leave it at that. If my Yanks win, you take me out to lunch…" Regina slipped him a sly smile. "…on a real date."

The Reds' batter swung and missed. Strike one.

Derek swallowed. "Wouldn't Josh be upset?"

Regina looked at him, confused. "Josh?"

"Josh Reinheart. Aren't you guys…like…a couple?"

Regina laughed. "Josh and me? Who told you that?"

"Nobody…I, well…you guys looked pretty friendly yesterday."

Regina shook her head, laughing some more. "Josh has been my older brother's best friend since they were in diapers. I've known him my whole life. I'm like his baby sister. I was just talking to him yesterday because my brother was home sick from school and, well…it was about…well, it's not really important."

Derek felt a wave of relief wash over him—*So she isn't going out with Josh after all! Maybe I, Derek Meyers, really do have a chance!*— but Regina looked suddenly uncomfortable. Derek decided to change the subject.

"He's there, you know," Derek said, gesturing at the television screen. "Josh is. At the game. He was bragging about it yesterday before baseball practice. His family scored tickets somehow."

"Yeah, they bought them weeks ago," Regina said absentmindedly. "Got eight, I think. Sold four of them to friends."

Derek suddenly thought of something. "Regina, I just realized...if your whole family is such Yankee fanatics, why aren't you all watching the game together? I mean, I'm surprised you're not having a party or something."

Regina looked away, embarrassed. A pause. Then:

"My family is at the game," Regina said, peering up at him through her bangs.

"What? There weren't enough tickets and you drew the short straw?" Derek said incredulously. He had never heard of anything more unfair in his life. Regina lived and died with her New York Yankees, just as he lived and died with his Cincinnati Reds.

"Actually, I was planning to go with them. Josh gave me the tickets yesterday. But then you asked me to come over and watch it with you...so I chose that instead."

Derek didn't think, just blurted out the first thing that popped into this mind: "WHY IN THE WORLD DID YOU DO THAT?"

Regina looked at him, surprised. This was not the reaction she had hoped for. "Well, because...well, isn't it obvious, Derek?" She blushed, looking down at her lap and winding that same loose string around her finger.

"I just—" Derek began, feeling his own cheeks glow. "I mean, I'm glad you came, Regina...but, wow, I can't believe it. You turned down a Worlds Series ticket...to watch the game on this crummy 36-inch non-plasma TV?"

"No," Regina said simply. "I turned it down to watch the game with you." She smiled, her green eyes meeting his brown ones. "Besides, they're awful nosebleed seats anyway."

*   *   *

Derek knew he was dreaming.

Not because Cincinnati was in Game 7 of the World Series, *thisclose* to being Champs. Not because Regina was sitting *thisclose* beside him on the couch, her knee gently touching his. Not even because she had been *thisclose* to watching the game in person at The Great American Ballpark, but instead decided to come over and watch it with him.

No, Derek knew he was dreaming because he was…

…rooting for the Yankees.

Yes, he was either dreaming or this was the end of the world. Things like this just don't happen. There are a few constants in life: breathing, eating, sleeping—and, for Derek, being a die-hard Reds fan. But now here he was, Derek Meyers, number-one-devoted-fan-since-the-day-he-was-born-and-his-parents-dressed-him-in-a-little-Cincinnati-Reds-baby-outfit, silently hoping New York would come out on top.

No, not because he was a Yankees fan. Because he was a Regina fan. He wanted that date with Regina so badly he was even willing to sabotage his own bet to get it.

If the Yankees win tonight, Derek silently pleaded to the Baseball Gods. *If the Yankees win tonight, I'll…*

Regina wiggled on the couch. "Strike two, Derek. Strike two!"

If the Yankees win tonight, I'll…

In the time between when the next delivery left the Yankee pitcher's hand and before it reached home plate, Derek realized something. He realized he didn't need upside-down stars. He didn't need the Baseball Gods. He didn't need a Yankees' victory to win a date or a Reds' victory to be a Champ. He didn't need to be the number-one fan of the number-one Championship team to be a Champ himself. He was already Champ.

So he did it. Just leaned in and did it. No wishes, no worries, no promises, no bets. Just a simple kiss that tasted like sweet victory. Like her smile. *Like a grand slam in the bottom of the ninth, when the crowd is going crazy but all you can hear is the beating of your heart…and you realize that this is what it truly means to be alive.*

He, Derek Meyers, was truly alive.

And Regina Phillips, the love of his high-school life, a Yankees fan, kissed him back.

HOO-BOY!

On the television screen, he could hear cheers erupting.

And the crowd goes wild!!!

A REAL BEAUTY

(Winner of the Let's Write Literary Contest)

The phone rings. Once. Twice. Then stops. After a brief silence—
one second, three seconds—it rings again.

The signal. Our secret code. I quickly pick it up and answer
without needing to hear the voice on the other end.

"Hi, Gramps! Had a feeling it was gonna be you."

"Did you see it tonight?" he asks.

I gaze out the window at the fiery streaks of orange and crimson
and purple brushed across the sky, outstretched fingers gradually
receding into the inky blackness. "Yeah, I sure did. It was a beauty,
wasn't it?"

"Certainly was. Yes indeed. A real beauty. It was almost as pretty
as the sunrise. Did you see that gorgeous one this morning?"

I laugh. Gramps is the only person I know who brews his cup of
coffee every morning to the sight of stars still dotting the California
sky outside his kitchen window. He has the entire morning paper
read and the crossword puzzle completed—in *ink*, for he's a brave
soul—by the time the sun rises to greet the rest of us. He is a
hard-core early bird. I, on the other hand, have always been a late

sleeper. Gramps knows this, yet he still always asks if I saw the sunrise. Always. It has become something of a running joke between us.

"No, gosh darn it! I missed it this morning," I say dramatically. "I guess I forgot to set my alarm for 5:30 a.m."

Gramps chuckles. "Yeah, well, you're a young one yet. Still a teenager. Old people like me, we enjoy getting up early. It's our nature. Just wait till your time comes, then you'll see."

"Yeah," I say, though I'm not sure I do agree. Deep inside, I don't really believe I'll ever grow old. It's too strange to think about. In my mind, I will always be young, strong, limber—full of life. Mom tells me all young people think they're immortal. Then one day, she says, you wake up and suddenly realize that you're not. It supposedly comes as a big shock. Out of the blue, you're old and getting up before the sun.

"So, how was school today?" Gramps asks. "Did you get your history test back?"

"Yeah, I got an A on it."

"That's my girl!" he says, and proudly.

"Thanks, Gramps. I must have gotten my brains from you."

"Aww, I don't know about that," he replies modestly. "Though I was always pretty good at history. It used to be my favorite subject in school. Fascinating, fascinating stuff. You like it too, don't you?"

"Uh-huh. But English is my favorite."

"Oh yeah, I knew that. You're the writer in the family. Just like Auden. She used to be an English teacher, did I ever tell you that?"

No, he hasn't. It's amazing, really, how little I know about my grandmother. Gramps doesn't talk about her too often. And when he does, I can never find the right thing to say to keep him going.

Like now. "Wow, Gramps, that's really…that's really cool," I stammer, after a moment's hesitation. I wish I had a way to let him know how much this little tidbit of information about her means to me. A way to tell him that now, whenever I do my English homework—study new vocabulary words, or read Robert Frost, or write an essay on the themes of *To Kill a Mockingbird*—I will think of her and my ordinary homework will suddenly become magical. That now, every day when I'm sitting in second-period Honors English I will try to imagine her up there writing on the board, teaching the class. That now, this part-of-me-that-was-once-a-part-of-her is almost sacred in my heart.

I wish I had a way to tell Gramps everything I'm thinking; a telepathic ray I could shoot from my mind to his. But I only have my own voice, and too often it falters trying to find the right words. So I just sit there, listening silently as Gramps goes on to describe the new high-tech Kitchen Aid mixer he bought at Kohl's today. I swear, my grandfather is addicted to that store. Mom jokes we have to put him on "shopping probation."

"Well, I just stopped by there to check things out because today is Wednesday, you know," he says. "And on Wednesdays they have a special senior citizen discount where all us old folks get fifteen percent off everything. Can you believe that? Fifteen percent off! I guess there are some perks to being an old guy like me, eh?"

"Yeah," I say. "They give you discounts at Kohls and you get to wake up early every morning and see the sunrise."

"It's a good life," he agrees. "It'd be perfect if Auden was still here, but at least I've got you, Dally."

"You...you've always got me, Gramps." I swallow. "Well, I should probably go. Homework to finish up."

"Oh, yes, yes, you go right along now," he says. It's like I said I have to attend a meeting with the President of the United States. To Gramps—top of his high school class who went to college on the G.I. bill and then to medical school—schoolwork is very important business.

"I'll talk to you tomorrow," I say.

"Okay. Listen, Dally, do you want me to call and wake you up in the morning? You know, so you can see the sunrise. It's gonna be a real beauty." I can almost *hear* him smiling.

"No, no, it's okay," I say, laughing a little. This is the second part of our joke. He always ends our conversations with this same question, even though he knows what my answer will be.

"Oh, you young people," he says with pretend exasperation. "Don't know what you're missing!"

"Well, you can describe it to me when I talk to you tomorrow?" I say. "I need my beauty sleep."

I smile as he tells me I'm the last person in the world who needs beauty sleep, just like he always does. One thing I love about grandparents is they make it seem like you are the most beautiful person in the world, simply because you are their grandchild and that's what grandparents do.

"Goodnight," I say. "Love and kisses."

"Love you too. Sleep tight," he replies.

I hang up the phone, take one last look out my bedroom window. The night has devoured all remnants of the sunset now; the sky is an endless expanse of inky-blackness. Not even stars show their faces tonight. I catch a glimpse of my own reflection as I stare out the window. Who is that girl? Sometimes I have an almost out-of-body experience, where it feels like I am standing off to the side, looking at myself, wondering who that person named Dallas Nicole is. I try to see myself as the kids at school do. *Oh, that's just Dallas,* they would say. *The quiet girl who sits by herself and reads all the time. She's really smart, you know. All she cares about is school.*

Except for a couple close friends, they do not know me at all. I am some other person around them, completely unlike the girl I am with Gramps. Sometimes it feels like I have a thousand different versions of myself floating around inside my soul. The trouble is, it's hard to tell which one is really me.

Who is that girl? The question hangs in the air, lingering like the last feeble rays of sunset. Then it, too, gets sucked up by blackness as I turn away from my half-reflection in the window. *Who is that girl?* I know the question-I-cannot-answer is not gone forever. Just like the sun will re-emerge in the morning, the question will also remain, lurking in the back of my mind to reappear another day.

I head over to my desk, scuffing my feet along my room's vacuum-deprived carpet. I wasn't lying; I do have homework to finish up. Not English tonight, though. Math.

*   *   *

The few memories I have of my paternal grandmother are scattered and vague, like pieces of a puzzle that don't quite fit together. Me sneaking up behind Auden in the kitchen and untying her apron strings, and her whirling around, pretending to be angry, and chasing me with hugs and kisses. Me snuggling beside her on the big couch as she reads me *Alice in Wonderland*. She giving me crushed ice in a cup to chew on as I help her water her roses. One time the automatic ice machine in the freezer door broke and ice splattered all over the kitchen floor. She just laughed and laughed, not angry in the least.

I'm not sure if these are actual memories or if they are just stories I've heard and convinced myself that I remember. I don't care either way, because at least they're something to go along with the photos of her and the beautiful quilt she made with squares cut from old jeans that covers my bed. Some of the jean squares even have actual pockets, and there is a tag—"Made with love by Auden." Sometimes I go over the memories in my mind at night when I'm having trouble falling asleep. I use my imagination to fill in the blanks. By now the images are so vivid it's as if a tiny film strip is playing behind my eyelids.

I have this one vivid image of her in my mind: bright red lipstick, short white curls, perfume smelling of roses and arms ready to envelope me in a hug. In my mind, she is always wearing a half-apron over a blue-checkered dress, and pearl earrings. She was very beautiful. Miss America beautiful, even. She was actually going to be in the pageant but declined, so she could marry Gramps sooner. He has a picture of her on their wedding day on the night-stand beside his bed. Breathtakingly beautiful. I think she would have won.

I know that she loved bowling and was a great dancer. Her mashed potatoes were the best you've ever tasted, and she always made chocolate truffles covered with chocolate sprinkles at Christmastime. Auden *loved* Christmas. Gramps would buy her one of those big white-flocked trees, tall enough to almost touch their twelve-foot living room ceiling. She decorated it from trunk to tree-top, and around it she piled the tons of presents she bought for all her children and grandchildren. She loved to shop for everyone but herself.

When I think of Christmas, that's what comes to mind. Chocolate truffles, a big white-flocked tree, and a mountain of brightly wrapped presents that soon became an even bigger mountain of wrapping paper. And she, beaming with joy, hugging everyone and taking pictures and bringing in new batches of truffles from the kitchen.

I was five when she died. Christmas hasn't been the same since. We all still get together, exchange gifts, try to keep up the traditions, but there's a quiet loneliness underneath all the festivities. I attempted to make chocolate truffles a few years ago, but they were a total disaster.

Now we just do without the truffles.

*   *   *

"Hey, Gramps."

"Hi, pun'kin. Did you see the sunset tonight?"

"Yeah, it looked like the sky was on fire!"

Gramps loved my grandmother more than anything in the world. When cynics say that love isn't real, I think of Gramps and Auden and smile. They loved each other more and more with each passing day, for thirty-eight years of marriage.

"So, how'd you do on that math test you were telling me about?"

"Fine. I got an A."

"That's my girl!"

They met in college on a blind date. He was a senior; she a sophomore. They were set up by a mutual friend, and went to a barn dance on Friday the Thirteenth. Gramps always says that superstition is just a bunch of baloney, because it was the luckiest day of his life.

It was love at first sight. They married and had three sons and a daughter. He took her out on "dates" often, and brought her flowers just because. Once the kids grew up and left home, Gramps and Auden traveled quite a bit. Hawaii, Mexico, the Caribbean, and even an Alaskan cruise. The week she died, they had just returned from a trip to Boston.

"So, Gramps, it's Wednesday. Did you go to Kohl's?"

"You betcha! I found this ginchy jacket. It's fleece, you know, really warm. Kinda like those ones they sell at Patagonia."

"Wow, it sounds like you scored a good deal! Have you tried out your new mixer yet?"

"Oh, yeah, I used it to make mashed 'taters last night…Not even close to as good as your grandma's were, though. She had a special touch."

"Yeah."

Auden thought she had the stomach flu the day she died. She was nauseated and very tired. The night before had been the forty-second anniversary of her and Gramps' first date, and they went out to dinner to celebrate. She assumed she had just eaten some bad seafood.

I mean, she was only sixty years old. But it wasn't bad seafood. It was a heart attack.

"Well, Gramps, I should probably go."

"Yes, yes, get that homework done! Atta girl. Do you want me to call you in the morning in time to see the sunrise? I bet it'll be a real beauty!"

"No, Gramps, it's okay. You can just describe it to me when I talk to you later."

"All right. Hey, did I ever tell you, Dallas, about your grandma being an early riser? She would have to wake *me* up to see the sunrise."

"No, Gramps, I…I never knew that."

Sometime past midnight, my grandmother got out of bed to get an antacid. Gramps heard a *thud* and rushed over to see if she was okay.

She wasn't. Gramps gave her CPR and called 911, but it was no use. I can't even imagine what it must have been like. Gramps kneeling beside her on the floor, staring at the love of his life who in a blink was gone forever. He, a veteran surgeon who has saved thousands of lives, not being able to do anything to save the one life that mattered most to him.

And downstairs on the kitchen table, sitting in a crystal vase of water she had filled, the still-fresh red rose he bought her on their first-date anniversary just two days before. Gramps had that rose preserved and keeps it in a case on his night stand, beside the picture of her on their wedding day. He sleeps with one of her sweaters under his pillow, because it still smells faintly of her perfume.

*   *   *

I open my eyes. It's still dark outside.

I've been tossing and turning all night—which is strange, because I rarely have trouble sleeping through the night. I grope for my watch, press the "night vision" button. 5:47.

I sit up, turn on the light. For some reason I don't even feel tired. It's like I've switched bodies with Gramps or something. I wonder if I'm getting old.

Yanking up the blinds, I see the sun beginning to rise. I watch as the streaks of pink and purple slowly overcome the darkness, waking up the world. A new day.

I check my watch again. October 15. And then I realize—today is the eleventh anniversary of Auden's death.

I imagine Gramps, my namesake—his middle name is Dallas— sitting at his kitchen table, probably just finishing up his crossword, bravely in ink, as always. I picture him looking out the window at the now vibrant sky and thinking of her. This is the hardest day of the year for him—no matter how many years pass, it doesn't get any easier. I wish I knew what to say, to let him know I understand, that I'm thinking of him and I'm sorry. And that I miss her, too.

But it seems my voice is never enough. *Who is that girl?* I'm always scared I'll say the wrong thing.

I pick up the phone and punch the seven digits I know better than my own phone number. Though nothing I say will ever bring Auden back, at least Gramps will know I care. And I suppose it's better to care and say the wrong thing than to not say anything at all.

I let the phone ring once, twice, and hang up. I sit there in silence for a moment, fingering the quilt she made and blinking away tears. Then I take a deep breath and dial again.

He picks up on the next ring.

"Hi, Gramps."

"Dally?"

"Yeah, it's me." I take a breath. Where do I go from here? What in the world am I supposed to do now?

I gaze out the window at the streaks of red sunrise fading into day. And for once I know exactly what to say.

"I actually woke up early enough to see the sunrise this morning, Gramps, can you believe it? And you're right—it sure is beautiful. Just like Auden. A real beauty."

About the Author

Dallas Woodburn is an eighteen-year-old graduate in the Ventura (California) High School Class of 2005. Her first self-published collection of short stories and poems, *There's a Huge Pimple on My Nose*, sold more than 800 copies and was praised in The Los Angeles Times: "If you simply want to enjoy some remarkable writing, it would be hard to find a book more satisfying than Dallas Woodburn's."

Dallas is a regular "Teen Talk" columnist for Family Circle magazine, which led to a January '05 guest appearance on The Early Show on CBS where she was interviewed by host Hannah Storm. Dallas has also been a featured author in the nationally-released books *So, You Wanna Be a Writer?*, *Good Friends Come Along Once in a Lifetime*, *Chicken Soup for the Teenage Soul IV*, *Chicken Soup for the Girl's Soul*, and *Chicken Soup for the Soul: The Real Deal on School*. In addition, she wrote the play her high school produced, and has been published in the national magazines Writer's Digest, Justine, Writing, Listen, Encounter, and The Hudson Valley Literary Magazine.

In 2000, Dallas founded a non-profit organization called "Write On!" that encourages kids to read and write through book drives and essay contests. (Check out Dallas's website at www.zest.net/writeon.) Her community work earned her the prestigious national 2004 Jackie Kennedy Onassis/Jefferson Award for "outstanding volunteerism," as well as a 2005 Congressional Award Gold Medal. Also in 2005, she was honored as a USA Today National Academic Team Member, a Ronald Reagan Presidential Library Scholar, and won Second Place in the national "Guardian Girls Going Places" contest.

When she's not writing, Dallas enjoys reading, sketching, hiking, white-water rafting, and watching chick flicks with friends. A four-year member of the Ventura High School cross-country team, she also enjoys running. Dallas will be a "Trustee Scholar" at USC as a freshman in the Class of '09 and plans to double-major in Creative Writing (surprise!) and Business.

978-0-595-35786-4
0-595-35786-5

Printed in the United States
84623LV00006BA/12/A

9 780595 357864